THE WILD ONE

The Wild One

BONNIE GOLIGHTLY

Includes a rare author profile and interview

"Bonnie Golightly: Author Still Living in the Shadow of Her
Name" by Wendi Watts is reprinted with permission from *The
Daily News Journal*, Sunday, August 30, 1998, © Wendi Watts –
USA TODAY NETWORK via Imagn Images.

This edition of *The Wild One* is published by Giant Books, which
reissues overlooked works by women writers. GiantBooks.org.

ISBN: 978-1-965751-16-9

Bonnie Golightly:
Author Still Living in the Shadow of Her Name
By Wendi Watts

Editor's note: This rare profile of Bonnie Golightly includes an extensive interview conducted shortly before her death. The article is reprinted with permission from the Lifestyles section of The Daily News Journal *of Murfreesboro, Tennessee, Sunday, August 30, 1998, © Wendi Watts – USA TODAY NETWORK via Imagn Images.*

Bonnie Golightly might have remained an enigma of Murfreesboro's past, but for a conversation at The Woman's Club last winter that set the memories of her in motion again.

While chatting at a December meeting of The Woman's Club, a member who had not grown up here commented on the number of literary connections in the community...Charles Egbert Craddock [pen name of Mary Noailles Murfree], Andrew Nelson Lytle, Andre Norton, Will Allen Dromgoole...

And a native of the city asked, "Have you heard of Truman Capote?"

"Yes, but what's the connection to Murfreesboro?" the newcomer naively asked.

'That Capote Thing'

The main character in Capote's short book "Breakfast at Tiffany's," which was turned into a movie starring Audrey Hepburn, may have been modeled on a woman who grew up in Murfreesboro.

The character, Holly Golightly, bears some striking similarities to the real woman, Bonnie Golightly.

The daughter of an MTSU professor of education, Bonnie grew up in the shadow of the university's campus from the mid-1920s to the mid-'40s. She went to dances and parties and was regularly mentioned in *The Daily News Journal*'s Partyline column.

Until recently, most of "the crowd" who used to hang out at the Golightly house at 1212 East Main St.—Susan Bragg, Kacky Holden, Charlotte Dill, Frances Nelson—thought Bonnie was dead. Others weren't sure. A few thought she was probably alive somewhere living as only Bonnie could.

To later generations, tales of her youth in Murfreesboro and later life in New York have been regarded as containing a grain of truth and a large measure folklore.

But Bonnie is very real and very much alive.

And she may forever be defined and, much to her chagrin, remembered mostly by one event that brought her national attention—what she refers to as "that Capote thing."

During World War II, Bonnie and her husband, Bob Sheffield, moved to Greenwich Village, where Bonnie owned and operated a bookstore called The Park Book Shop. She later divorced Sheffield but continued living and working in the city.

At the same time, Truman Capote was living in New York and making a name for himself as a writer. Among his most famous works set in that era is the novella *Breakfast at Tiffany's*.

Holly Golightly was the story's main character, a charming 19-year-old cat lover with an aversion to attachments of any kind—a wild thing not meant to be held down by social conventions.

Holly's fictional life and Bonnie's real one shared many similarities—growing up in the South, living in a brownstone on Manhattan's East Side with a bar around the corner on Lexington, singing folk music, having an assortment of dramatic and theatrical friends and acquaintances and having a love of cats.

"I knew an awful lot of people who knew Capote," Bonnie said in a recent telephone interview from her home in New Haven, Conn. "I did not know Capote at all, and he denied all of his life that he had based the book on me. After he died…somebody admitted in *New York Magazine* that he had based the whole thing on me."

Capote "knew somebody who knew me very well, a bitch, who really bitched the hell out of me," the 79-year-old recalled. "She was somebody who, she thought she had taken away my boyfriend. My boyfriend returned to me and she really had it in for me from then on. And I got backlash for years, *years*. She apparently talked to Capote and Capote didn't know I still lived in New York or anything else, and he thought he was perfectly safe in using my name.

"I first heard about this from a friend, David Lubis, also a writer—a published writer—who lived in an apartment I had lived in a few months before.

"Christmastime came and I dropped by the apartment to see if I'd gotten any mail and he said, 'Oh, I didn't know you existed!' And I said, 'What do you mean?' And he told me he had heard Capote read from a work in progress…and the name [of the main character] had been Connie Golightly. 'Connie,' for constantly traveling.

"And so I said, 'I'm not going to put up with this,' and called up Hiram Haydn…somebody I knew at Random House [publishing company], and said, 'Please don't let Capote use my name.'"

Bonnie was told the name "Golightly" had been used before in literature and was not unheard of as the name of a character.

"But…from what I had been told about the work in progress, there were too many similar things," Bonnie explained. "I just didn't want it. And I especially didn't want it because I was a writer myself and I didn't want him to use my name.

"So Hiram went to Capote, who agreed to change the name, and the name was changed to 'Holly Golightly,'" Bonnie said, and added with more than a tinge of sarcasm in her voice, "Big deal."

Breakfast at Tiffany's was published by Random House in 1958 and appeared in *Esquire* magazine the same year.

Bonnie was so outraged, she filed libel and invasion of

privacy lawsuits asking for $800,000 against Capote, *Esquire* and Random House, according to an article in *Time* magazine.

The *Time* article appeared in the Feb. 9, 1959, issue and said, Capote "claims that his Holly had three 'counterparts in reality,' none of them Bonnie. 'One of them is dead—she died in Africa, the other two are very much alive and have no intention of suing me.'"

Capote also is quoted in response to Bonnie's lawsuit as saying, "I have never met nor seen this lady…. It's ridiculous for her to claim she is my Holly."

Capote never publicly revealed whom he based the character of Holly Golightly on, but a number of women who knew the author have seen themselves in her. Author Doris Lilly, novelist Pati Hill, artist Beatrice Whistler [Dabney] and actress Carol Grace all claim to have been his inspiration, according to information posted on an Internet site about *Breakfast at Tiffany's*.

But Bonnie claims she paid a high price for Capote's work because she shared her last name with his character.

"It really semi-ruined my writing life," Bonnie says. "I'm not kidding you…. I was advised by publishers to change my name. I had become a figment of [Capote's] imagination…. It was very discouraging, first of all. It made me feel as if I were a bird that had its wings pulled off…. Afterward, I didn't write very much on my own. I wrote mostly things that editors would come to me and ask me to write for them."

Bonnie's lawyer dropped the lawsuit.

The Capote incident is still a thorn in Bonnie's side, and she continues to fight to have her writing and contributions to the body of American literature recognized, contributions her friends from childhood had no doubt Bonnie would make.

Memories of Murfreesboro

Born June 23, 1919, in Chicago to Thomas J. and Emily Rogers Golightly, Bonnie was their second child. Her brother, Thomas Jr., was seven years older.

When Bonnie was an infant, the family moved to North Dakota.

In 1925, the family moved to Murfreesboro, where her father joined the faculty at Middle Tennessee Normal College. Bonnie began her formal education at Campus School in what is now known as Kirksey Old Main on the MTSU campus.

Among her first-grade classmates was Susan Lytle, now the wife of John Bragg, retired state representative.

"I knew her all the way through school," Susan recalled. "She wrote quite a bit. I can remember her sitting in class and not paying a bit of attention because she was writing short stories. And she was good…. Even in grade school, she came and did what she wanted. I guess that's what made her different.

"She was very independent. She had a good mind, but she didn't care about school at all," Susan continued. "I can still see her in English class with a tablet just writing up a storm…. She had no discipline. If she liked you, she was a friend. She could tell you off if she wanted to."

Even as a child, Bonnie knew she wanted to be a writer.

"Everybody in my family wrote," she recalled. "I started writing when I was 8 years old. I wrote stories…things about playmates. You know, silly little things."

After completing grammar school at Campus, Bonnie attended Central High School.

During these years, the Golightly home was the regular meeting place for Bonnie's friends and acquaintances.

"I had an awful lot of friends in Murfreesboro," Bonnie said. "We had a 'crowd' as we called it. There were about 10 of us in the crowd. Susan was one of them. Emily Crichlow, Juanita Highman… We'd meet after school, largely, and then at night, too, on weekends. We always had parties on weekends, very often at my house…. I don't know why it was…. I had my own car when I was 14, a Willys-Knight roadster with a rumble seat, apple green. Very cute car."

One of the reasons the Golightly house was such a popular spot was that Bonnie's parents were more permissive than most in Murfreesboro at that time, members of the crowd explained.

"The [Golightly] household was not quite run like anyone else's in Murfreesboro," Susan said. "There were no restrictions."

"The gang seemed to go to her house on Friday nights," recalled Charlotte Dill, another member of the crowd. "I guess we liked to go there because Bonnie wouldn't let her mother and daddy bother us."

But all of Bonnie's memories of growing up in Murfreesboro are not happy.

"They used to say that it had 10,000 people," Bonnie said. "Actually, there were 7,900. Everybody knew everybody. I mean, there were people one simply did not know. You knew their names; that was it. It was a very snobby place. It was just awfully snobby. When the Cotillion Club was formed, a lot of really nice people got blackballed for no good reason. Meanness.

"My parents were older than my friends' parents, so my parents did not socialize with my friends' parents, so it made sort of a gap. But I was never top drawer really. I was secret top drawer.... It was a complicated thing."

Bonnie did not want to stay in Murfreesboro. She didn't know where she wanted to go, but she did know what she wanted to do.

Since she was a child, Bonnie longed to be a writer.

"Our house was right on the edge of town in those days," Bonnie said. "The city limits were about a half mile away from 1212 E. Main St. And I used to sit on the front steps and think, 'I really don't want to go North, but look at all those interesting cars going by.... I really don't want to stay here, but I don't want to go North.'"

Experiences in Literature

North, though, is where she ended up when she married Bob Sheffield, one of her father's students at the university. Bob had grown up in New York and Connecticut.

The couple moved to New York, where Bonnie opened

and operated Park Book Shop from 1943-48. The shop specialized in out-of-print and rare editions.

From 1949-53, she was assistant manager at Hacker Art Books at Hacker Art Gallery.

Since 1954, she has been a freelance writer and editor, currently working as an editor with *Writer's Digest*.

"I knew an awful lot of people, but I didn't know them well," she explained. "I'm one of those people who can name drop and name roll, but that's about it. I didn't have close associations with most of them…. [Poet and author] William Carlos Williams was the only one I knew very, very well in that group. I met an awful lot of his friends too. But I knew him quite well.

"He was living in Rutherford, N.J., at the time. But he came into New York frequently as people do in New Jersey and Connecticut. They come into the city for one reason or another. And I met him because I had read something called *In the Money*. He wrote three novels, and that's one of them. And I wrote him a fan letter. He came by the shop and was fascinated. So, we became friends, and he and Josie, his wife, invited me to their house by the bay, and I would go out there frequently. And William game me copies of all his books.

Bonnie became an author in her own right. She has penned 20 books, including novels, mysteries, gothic fantasies and romances. She also did novelizations of movies such as *Legend of the Lost*, *The High Cost of Loving*, and *Olympia* for Avon book publishers.

During her writing career, she has used the pen names Milton Rogers, her maternal grandfather's name, and Helen

Sheffield.

Her most successful books have been *Shades of Evil*, a mystery, and *The Wild One*, a novel about an upper-class teenager who falls in and out of love with an older man.

Her first novel was based on a memory of Murfreesboro.

"The first novel I wrote was about…an incident down in the bottoms [in Murfreesboro]." Bonnie said. "I don't know if you still call it the bottoms or not, near the river. Poor people lived there.

"And there was a little boy who had a wolf on a chain, and I saw this wolf. We used to drive around all the time. It's one of the things we'd do…and I'd see this wolf on this chain and that was the basis of my first novel, which nearly got published."

Her favorite work is the last one published, titled *Polly Paris*, a gothic tale now out of print.

"I wrote eight books before I ever got published," Bonnie said. "I didn't get published until the early '50s. And I never would have gotten published, I suppose, except for having connections. That's the only way you really get ahead in this damn business…. I had a friend who worked for Avon books, and she commissioned the first book."

Among the books she wrote for Avon are *Beat Girl*, *The Intimate Ones* and *The Integration of Maybelle Brown*.

The last book she wrote, *The Veil of Order*, was about memories of Murfreesboro. It remains unpublished.

"I wrote that for myself," Bonnie said. "It nearly got published countless times. And it got to the point an editor would call and say, 'Let's have lunch,' and I'd say, 'Are you going to publish my book?' They'd say, 'Let's talk about it.' And I'd say, 'No thank you,' because at least 20 times that happened."

The 1,200-page book "was about Murfreesboro and made-up stuff about the South…. It's really not about Murfreesboro per se. There was nobody in it identifiable. But it was an amalgam. It was a saga opening in the late 19th century and went up to 1946, I think, something like that. There were similarities to people I knew."

Bonnie produces her work on a typewriter and never revises.

"I sit down and I write until I drop," Bonnie explained. "The longest I think I ever wrote without really stopping except to get up and answer the phone or open a can of soup was 125 pages."

That was a 12-hour write-a-thon.

She has the plots for her stories in her head.

"And then, the voices talk to me and tell me what to say, I've always said," Bonnie said. "It's a ridiculous kind of way to characterize it, but that's pretty much the truth…. But I simply cannot revise. I have tried, and I ruin it every time I try."

When inspiration strikes, she usually starts writing immediately.

"If I get interrupted, it's usually forever," Bonnie said. "The long book, *The Veil of Order*, I got interrupted and it took me, I think, a couple of years before I finally finished it. It just died on the vine."

She added that writers have their own preferences in how they create their work.

"Writing is such an individual thing that you can hardly characterize that it should be this way or that way or the other way," she said. "It's whatever way it comes out. That's the best advice to give any writer."

Her days now are filled with reading, writing and taking care of the six cats who share her home in New Haven—three inside, three out.

What does she plan to write in the future?

"I don't know," Bonnie replied. "I guess, I just…thought I had something to say, and one of the reasons I don't write much anymore is that I don't have anything to say."

*

Maybe so.

But her old chums at Murfreesboro's Woman's Club, where Bonnie's mother was once a member, have plenty to say about their friendships with Bonnie Golightly. And they are certain the book will never close on their memories of the wild young girl who will always live in the shadow of her name.

THE WILD ONE

PART ONE

I

"Youth is all sex," my mother is fond of saying. "It's exciting for a while, but eventually tiresome." Then she admits, with one of her languorous, studied sighs, that she never should have had children; should indeed have "waited forever" as her friends said she did anyhow.

"Phallic" and "compulsive" and "Freudian"—all those words—were like mother's milk to me, and my mother never lets anyone forget that she out-Irised Iris March in *The Green Hat*, and that Scott Fitzgerald once said to her that she was the real prototype of Daisy in *The Great Gatsby*. I knew all about these people long before I knew about any real ones. My brother Bart and I entered the world practically wearing raccoon coats, waving pennants and drinking "booze" out of flasks. Our problem was not growing up, but growing down to size.

Maybe if our father hadn't died when Bart was nine and some seven months before I was born, mother would have let us grow up like children instead of like Jack-the-Giant-Killer plants that she forgot to water more often than she remembered. We were both stunted in one way and precocious in another, and neither of us had many friends to begin with, for like does indeed seek like and we were only like each other, even though we were so many years apart. That's one of the reasons Joycie was so important to me. Next to Bart, she was most important, because Mother, winsome and lovely as she sometimes was with us, always had her new husbands to look after. Daddy was her second and there were two others after him. Both dreadful.

It's no wonder that Mother, having been through that many weddings, doesn't think too much of them. She was between husbands again when Joycie and Bart decided to get married; but that still doesn't explain the stand she took. At first she didn't seem to mind, for though she had said some awfully snide things about the Bradfords, she had always been fond of Joyce. However, danger flares began to shoot up after Joyce and Bart actually announced the wedding plans. And that morning before the wedding was really the end.

We were all having coffee together in the den. I was delirious with happiness, literally, so maybe that's why I made that stupid remark about their wedding being a happy ending to a very Grimm fairy tale. "Or maybe it's only the beginning," Mother remarked calmly. I suppose she resented the slip I had made, still, our lives *had* been rather grim. Anyway, ten seconds later she flatly refused to go to the wedding. "Don't worry," she told Bart before he could splutter a protest. "You'll have plenty of others, I'm sure." And that was that.

I went out in the hall, as Bart asked me to so he could talk to her, and I found to my surprise that it really is true about aching with misery. I was as wracked with physical pain as if Mother had suddenly died, and I sat there stricken all morning—while those two ranted and roared at each other, "keening," as Kathleen called it when she came up from the kitchen—

When it got to be noon, everybody, all the servants—Kathleen, Tony, Jess and Tennie—Bart, Mother, and I knew she wouldn't go; that no matter how long he stayed in there with her Bart and I would end up driving to Connecticut all by ourselves, making phony excuses for her to the Bradfords, going through all the motions of the rehearsal party and everything as if her absence were due to a natural calamity, not caused by caprice.

Sitting there through those hours, all packed and ready (as I had been for at least two days), I tried to think back over it all: why had she done this to Bart and Joycie—to me—to herself? Only it was hard to think with all the racket that was going on, for the infection had spread: downstairs in the kitchen Kathleen was having another row with Tennie, and I knew pretty soon Jess and Tony would get into it too. Once last summer we had to call the police. Our house is rather like the music department at school when everyone is practicing different instruments and different scales at the same time. Only here people exercise their tempers. School. It was a long cool thought that morning, and I longed for it like a friend; just the way I longed to rush to the phone and tell Joycie, my friend, all about what a beastly thing Mother was doing. Only

I couldn't.

Whenever I'm miserable I try to think of quiet, cool things—waterfalls and swimming pools, shade trees and sitting under them on the grass, drinking something icy that tinkles in a tall glass, my dead grandmother's drawing room in Baltimore in the summer when the shutters were closed against the afternoon sun, and yes, today, even school. I would be going back there on Monday for Commencement, after this nightmare was over. Miss Chalmers' seemed such a small island of misery this early June morning, compared with the continent of misery that was home. Then I thought of Pritchard Allyn, but that wasn't a cool thought, and I had promised myself after those two letters he couldn't be bothered to answer, never to think of him again. Maybe that's how I came to think about the Indian vase.

It was ancient, of course, made of black basalt, and had belonged to my father. I hadn't noticed it for a long time, but there it was, still on top of that broken-down old Empire chest with the inlay working out like bad teeth; it made Tennie grumble every time she had to polish it. For years, I remembered, the vase had somehow been a phallic symbol to me—probably from the time I first heard the word—but I had long since ceased to notice it, for it had just blended into the familiar forest of furniture.

Now I gave it a good look. Had Daddy, as Bart still called him because he had known him, dug it up himself? He had been interested in archaeology, had spent summers, when he was at Harvard, digging in Mexico, but he had ended up on Wall Street—a long way that was from Aztecs and plumed serpents…poor dead guy. Then I thought of something else, a thing I had written last year for Creative Writing: "You can't expect me to live *here*," says Life, so it quits and goes away. Maybe I had had him in mind, though the grade I got on that thought was negligible.

But why had Daddy died? Of course he was lots older than Mother, although she was forty herself when I was born. I think he must have been about sixty, when he died, or almost. That meant he would be nearly seventy-seven now. And my grandmother (Mother's mother), who was only five years older, would be eighty-two. It made me feel like a small green branch on a dead tree—a queer, lonely feeling.

I suppose I must have been crying again, though I didn't know it, for Tennie came up suddenly, crying herself, and put her arms around me. "Oh, Miss Chloe! Can't nobody make that stubborn thing do nothing. That Miss Cornelia ain't going. I know her by heart." Tennie really did know my mother, but really. She had been with her family in Baltimore, been with her all her life, so to speak; or, as my mother would say to explain Tennie's presence in the household, "She's been with me all my awful life."

"You go set in the car," Tennie told me. "I'll go on in there in a few minutes and tell Mr. Bart to come on and y'all get started. Miss Joycie and them must be having a fit."

"No," I said. "I'm going to talk to her myself."

Tennie moaned at this and shook her head. "You go on down and get in that car 'cause it ain't no use what nobody says. She's got that mean mind all made up." She went away sobbing and wiping her eyes. It made a chill go through me.

Tennie was absolutely right, but I was stubborn too: I *would* talk to my mother; I had to.

Only what could I say? You're spoiling everything, your clothes are all packed and ready, why won't you come? No, Bart had said all that hours ago—I had heard him. He had dragged in my long friendship with Joyce, his pride, her pride, their pride, everything—only Daddy's pride remained. Daddy would hate you for this. Yes, I could say that.

I looked at the vase. When I was awfully little, before I had thought it was a phallic symbol, I dimly remembered being afraid of it. I had thought then that it was a funeral urn holding my father's ashes. I had even prayed to it once or twice. I had been a really psycho kid and even Mother had been worried about me, sent me to a psychiatrist and all that for a while. But I had probably gotten the funeral-urn idea from her, because in those days I had confused her private myths with other fairy tales, just as I confused my new fathers with new men who came around. When I was very little Mother liked poetry a lot: Rupert Brooke and Alan Seegar and that Flanders Field thing about the first big war—all, I realized afterward, years too late; just as she was too late with the Rilke, Baudelaire kick that followed. And then her paint-ing—after Salvador Dali and surrealism were a dead issue, she took up Max Ernst. That was what was wrong with my mother: she flipped over things exactly when everybody else was finally giving them up. Now she was painting like D. H. Lawrence, or so said the few reviews she got. Her last show had been a debacle but she kept on having exhibitions be-cause there were always dealers willing to take on those who could pay.

Aunt Maude, my father's sister, always said she was going to leave me a lot of money because Mother would certainly have none left to leave. Of course Bart had his own income—which sometimes made Mother fairly furious—because he was here when Daddy was, but I was a post-mortem addition. I used to think, about the same time I believed Daddy's ashes were in the vase, that Mother had gotten me mixed up with somebody else's child in the hospital; but then I knew I was wrong, because she hadn't wanted to choose any baby from the selection they showed you in the hospital (that's where I thought babies came from, in those days). But maybe it wasn't her fault. Maybe her life was awful. Maybe that was why she drank too many martinis too many nights; maybe that was why the Bradfords would believe us when we had to tell them, if we ever got there to tell them, that is, that she was sick. My mother, I knew, was a crazy mixed-up kid if ever there was one. Maybe that was why she was doing this wretched thing.

I got up and walked around—paced, really—and thought about Mother in there in the den, playing solitaire while she argued with Bart, looking at the cards, not at him, when she made her rebuttals, for the most part quietly, but screaming at him when she felt she had to to make her point. It was maddening. Why didn't he come out so I could talk to her? Poor hurt Mother. Why was she doing it? If only I had a *real* father! A procession of not-fathers and near-fathers sat on her dressing table upstairs—all the men in her life except my own father, whose portrait, by what my mother called "an earnestly eclectic ass," hung in the library. When she got drunk she would commune with these pictures, talk to them, upbraid them. Sometimes she would tell me about them. "They were awful, Chloe, awful. And I had them all. No sir. No more flappers in this house. I'll keep you sweet and innocent. Never know them all."

I hadn't known then what she meant. But maybe I did now, even if I hadn't "known" anybody and if Pritchard was the nearest I had ever come to it.

But love, I knew, was sweet, or could be. Joyce and Bart had fallen in love very gently. Almost without knowing. Just as I imagined my mother had fallen in love with my father. Joyce had been around—underfoot, as Bart used to say—for years. Then suddenly there she was. And my mother had known my father in Baltimore when she was my age; he had been a friend of her favorite uncle. They had fallen in love gently. Story-book love. The best. Why, why couldn't she see that Bart's was like hers?

Just then Bart came tearing out. "Let's go," he said and jammed on his new straw hat. But Mother was standing in the doorway, looking at me with that peculiar tight-lipped glittering smile that is mostly in her eyes.

"I want to talk to Chloe," she said. "Just for a minute. You won't be so very late."

I tried to think of what I had been going to say—it had been about Daddy, how she had to come not just for us, but because of him. I don't know what happened to that speech. I was on my feet, smiling back at her, glad to have a chance to say what I had to say and everything, when suddenly my eye moved over to that Indian vase again, that phallic symbol. Phallic, phallic, phallic, and all of a sudden I remembered why I had begun to think of it as that. It was one morning right after I had started going to school, and Tennie had hurried, dressing me, because I was late. Then she shoved me downstairs and kept shoving me through the hall. Just before we got to the door to the den, which was open, she began to hurry me even more, but I stopped anyway in surprise, for there stood a strange man, not one of the daddys, or anybody, naked, and inside on the couch was Mother, naked too, stretching out her hand and saying something like, "darling, let's have another cigarette and some of that gin over there...." And even as Tennie rushed me on, I had caught a glimpse of the Indian vase out of the corner of my eye and the strange dark-fleshed man seemed just like it....

As I thought about this now, Mother's face blurred, and I was turning away, shaking my head. She followed us down to the entrance, talking all the time, to me. I don't know what she said. But I didn't say anything. I knew there was really nothing to say. Knew it for the first time. Daddy hadn't been true and gentle love for her, nobody had. Everything had just been an Indian vase, so it was better that she stayed at home and kept out of Bart's and Joycie's wedding.

II

Even in the car, I don't think I realized how much on to
my mother I was just then, or how much I hated being parted
so suddenly from her and from innocence. I felt laid bare. I
couldn't say anything to Bart, and he, of course, had nothing
to say to me. He was going through his version of what had
happened in his own mind—a mind nine years older. It suddenly seemed miraculous to me that he and Joyce were going
to be married. And for the first time it also seemed terrible,
sickening, to me. What was going on anyway? Swathed in
childhood, I still remained, brought up by careful Tennies
and Kathleens and Aunt Maudes, sitting in famous austere
restaurants all over the world, looking at the world from my
highchair, my legs dangling, listening to the crisp and witty
Cornelias, not having the least idea what a martini meant. No
wonder Pritchard had whispered in my ear that I was "so
young and soft"!

I can't say the Indian vase did it, of course. Neither that
nor the cautious year in England with Aunt Maude nor the
year at that place in France when she flew over every weekend. And New York hadn't done it either, not being at school
at Miss Chalmers' where I had leaned heavily on knowing

everything and understanding nothing. Joyce and I both had. But was Joycie like that too? She was so quiet. Maybe so dumb. I had never once thought of her that way before. It seemed she always just listened to me, to everybody, then giggled. What did she really know? What was she really doing marrying my brother Bart? Why, why, had I never said out loud to myself that it was all funny, that I hadn't thought anything, didn't know anything? Memorizing T. S. Eliot didn't teach one to understand. Nothing did. I was wide open.

I felt wild, like screaming, getting out and tearing New York City apart with my bare hands. I was as giddy as if I were drunk, and I'd seen drunk people that way. Lots of them at my mother's parties. Only I had always thought of them, watching them, as smart people who hurt too much to stand it, and so who got drunk in order to be stolid and impervious. Now I knew it was something else. That day before Joyce's wedding, I was alive, grown-up. And I would be seventeen in the fall. It was not a moment too soon.

Bart's car was wide open too. It matched me. It was a white Caddy convertible which Mother had given him on his twenty-fifth birthday. So it wasn't new, but it looked it because he hated it and never drove it. He walked to his office on Madison Avenue. Fifteen blocks every day, starting at eight-thirty in the morning, and always getting there before anyone else he knew. He was an account executive in the advertising firm where he had started as a messenger in the mail room right after he got out of Harvard. That was how he'd wanted it. I don't think anybody there knew he was Bart

Longtree III. They all thought he was just a bright college boy who had made his way. He never mentioned his work at home or brought anybody from the office for drinks or dinner.

This was one of the things with Bart and me: we both thought reality was awfully unreal. I wondered, looking at his profile (he had Aunt Maude's sleek, beautiful nose) what people thought of him in his office, and I wondered too what they thought of me at school. But who was there at school to think, really think, I mean? There was sort of Avery Stafford. Sometimes she went with me and Joyce to Schrafft's for a hot fudge sundae. But the rest of them were just last names, just classmates. Only for the last two years I had been a boarding student, even though our house was only ten blocks away from the school, because Mother had been abroad so much, and I had had Portia Bleeker for a roommate. Portia Bleeker, Avery Stafford...I looked at the East River.

We were driving fast and the tears had dried on my face. The early summer air was hot, portentous of real summer. We would soon be off the East River Drive onto the Parkway. I hadn't even noticed when we hit the Drive. Anyway, now I looked at the water. I hadn't seen the East River in days. The water was quilted, delicate. Sometimes it would rise up into caps, lace caps, with the water underneath like green satin dresses on frenzied dancing figures. Up in Connecticut there might be lots of that, for Joyce had an older sister who was great for dances. This was the summer Joyce had planned to come out. How I had dreaded it! Then, I had thought, I would be all alone. All alone until next year when I was to come out. I froze again as if I'd had the idea mentioned to me for the first time. I'm not ready, I'm not ready! That's what I had thought when Mother and I talked it over a few months ago. And I had put off thinking about it—after all I didn't *know* anybody, who would I ask? Could that be why I was glad, or had been glad, that Joyce was going to miss all that, would be married instead? Joycie married! The thought scooped me out, left me empty. She wouldn't be Joyce Bradford any more. She wouldn't be going back to Chalmers. Only I would.

"Wind too much for you, Mole?" Bart asked me. His voice was as sad as a funeral. We were hours late. What was he thinking? Well, certainly he was, at the moment anyhow, thinking of me. He had called me "Mole," and that meant something. It had been his name for me since the days when I used to hide in Mother's closet during her parties and someone always had to come dig me out. "I'll put up the top," he said, and I could tell he was worried.

"Don't," I told him. "I like it." I tried to give him one of my big smiles, but it just came out tawdry-brave. We still weren't ready to talk to each other, and those awful tears came again. My eyes were like open wounds. But realization that day had beaten me flat; like an exhausted swimmer on the beach, waves and waves of it poured over me, pounding me into the deserted stretch of sand. There was no one, I knew, I could talk to: Bart was gone, if he had ever been there, and Joyce, who *had* been there, was gone too. They were like lost voices calling to me: I could answer, but they couldn't hear.

For the first time in my life, I really tried to plan ahead. What would I do this summer? What, as a matter of fact, would I do when I went back to school? I knew their questions, everybody saying "Sister of the groom, oh, sweetie! Tell us all about it—did Joyce look like an angel? Had they made out before, do you think? Did you get bombed on champagne and all that other stuff?" And I knew I would answer, Yes, yes, yes. What else?

But I had never been "bombed" on anything, nor had I "barfed" or any of the other things people like Avery Stafford talked about. I had lived at school, wherever it was, London, France, Switzerland, New York, and I had gone home for holidays, wherever home was, and I had listened. Only what I had heard, however fascinating, had fallen, I knew, on an untrained ear. I didn't even know, for instance, if Bart had ever been drunk in his life; I had never thought to ask.

"Do you mind," Bart was saying, "if I tell them that we were late because of you?"

I was surprised. "Why me?"

"What else can I say?" he asked.

I thought about it. Why couldn't he say we were late because of something he did, or that the car did? This was an old puzzle, really. Often he had asked my permission to use me as an excuse for some defection. Usually I didn't mind. Why did I mind today? I thought about his voice, lonesome as the blues. He was haunted and miserable. Both of us were. Mother sat, as surely as if she had come along, between us on the seat. A living wraith, a flower wreath, a virago, a charm, a banshee, an angel—Cornelia Mabry Marlowe Longtree

Atkins O'Shea. Not really pretty ever, with her thin dark hair and rather funny nose, but "marvelous," "talented," "ingenious"—said the many, many who were taken in. But eventually, most of them were "let out" for thinking otherwise. "What did she say to you?" I asked, my voice breathless, almost a whisper, because I didn't want to know as much as I did.

"It's funny," he said, "but I can't really remember. She mostly just said she was too hung over to go through it all."

"—And no reflection on you and Joyce?"

"No reflection on us. She couldn't make it. Said she might drive up tomorrow, except then she remembered it was Tony's day off."

I pulled my coat up around my ears; that shut out the sounds of traffic at least. I wanted to reach out and take Bart's hand. But he was watching the road again, and his part of the interrogation was, it seemed, finished. After all, it was Bart who was taking the positive step, and it struck me for the first time that our mother's absence at his wedding meant much less to him than it did to me.

And, what after all did her absence mean? A social error? That aspect of it no doubt bored her. A slap in the faces of her children? What was another slap? Then I knew, as I had known all the time: it was jealousy, little-girl, mean, nasty jealousy.

Joycie wasn't a "late child," you see. Her mother, Ida Bradford (she had been Ida Ramsey), was only forty something now, and her father too. My mother called them "awful young people," always had, even when she said in the next breath how fond she was of Joycie. She called Mrs. Bradford a "great big brute of a girl," but I know she was jealous of her, for Mrs. Bradford is still a "glamour girl," which is what Mother used to say Joyce would be when she grew up—very tall, good body, good eyes, dark hair, and fresh peach skin. As a matter of fact, Mother couldn't go to Ida Ramsey's coming-out party because Bart was born that night. And later it seems Mother was mixed up with Henry Bradford, or so Aunt Maudie used to say when I stayed with her in England, even though he was a lot younger than she. I think Mother never forgave Ida Bradford for marrying him. She had certainly been vicious about her as long as I could remember. "That woman spends her entire life in bed," she once said. "Either she's making babies, having babies, or recovering from one or the other. She's a sow. She's nothing. Ask Tennie. Tennie knows. Or better still, ask Kathleen. Kathleen is Irish. She knows the Irish. She told me once when Ida was here that she didn't like waiting on people of her own class…." Maybe it was Bart who reminded her that Ida Ramsey Bradford was English, that Kathleen, if she had said such a thing, must have meant somebody else. But Mother's mind was made up. She was jealous of Ida, despite the fact that after all the childbearing which Mother made so much of, only two of her children survived. The twins had died of polio and Joyce's brother had been killed in the Korean War.

Perhaps Mother, somewhere in inner wistfulness, wished she had had more of us. She had carried the child-bearing project to its completion only twice, though she had been offered the same opportunity probably more times than she could count and had declined by means of any number of discreet legal abortions. The word "abortion" was another of my childhood favorites. Bart, she always said, was a "love" child. Before, I had thought that meant she loved my father and that I had been a "love child" too, but today I rather thought that she meant instead she had "loved" the idea of being a mother, and that by the time I came along she was bored with it.

"Somehow I thought I knew her," Bart mused aloud.

"So did I," I said.

"I thought she would come. I didn't think she would do this to me."

It stunned me. He had said "to me," not "to us," which would have meant everybody. I wondered about him. Did I really know him, this brother of mine? Yet we had been so close, in spite of distance in age or miles. I had written him every week when I hadn't seen him. I had grown up on his letters. Hadn't he grown up on mine, or was he grown already, self-sufficient, planted, before mine ever came?

But then I was sorry. It was to him that she had done the worst thing of it, and he suffered, suffered horribly. No matter if she had done dreadful things to my best friend; my mother had done dreadful things to my brother's wife. That was everything! Joyce was going to be his wife! I felt myself rise up inside as if I'd been on a bobsled; in a minute I would be plunging down.

"God, Mole," he said, "I need a drink. How about you? Have you ever had a drink in a tavern with a man?"

I hadn't. I was going to tell him about it, but just then we pulled up to pay a Parkway toll.

"Thanks for nothing," Bart muttered as we drove away, out of earshot of the toll collector who thanked us. Then he was silent, and a long time later he saw a place, and said, "There's a drink. Think you can take it, Mole?" He pulled off the side of the road, and parked in a great hurry.

"I certainly hope so," I said, but I don't think he even heard me.

III

Even entering the grounds, I would have known there was a wedding on. The message fairly sang from the trees, the lawns. Caterers seemed to be everywhere, for it was to be a lawn wedding tomorrow, in a bower, and the rector who had married Joyce's grandparents was going to marry her and Bart. All of her first cousins were going to be in the wedding, and her sister Lesley was going to be maid of honor, which is why I was just asked along as a spectator.

My mother had made much of this, even when she had still been guarded about her disdain for their marriage. And to tell the truth, I was a little hurt. Surely one cousin could have been left out. But the Bradfords took family relationships very seriously. Somehow I felt that after Joyce and Bart were married, I would be more firmly entrenched than ever. Then I too would be almost one of the family.

For I loved the Bradfords; everything about them. Even when they still kept that topsy-turvy apartment in town, which they did until Joyce was thirteen or so, I had loved any place they inhabited. I didn't care if it was "rather filthy and extremely tacky," as my mother said in disgust after having gone there once for cocktails. I loved it.

I felt the same way about their house in Connecticut. After they decided to live out there the year round, my mother began calling them the "Bucolic Bradfords," declaring that her one visit there had caused her to come down with "milkleg," even though their place lacked any bovine aspect. It was some miles out from New Canaan and had once been a farmhouse but was one no longer. It was a sprawling place surrounded by totally uncultivated acreage, though all of it was more or less tended and cut back. It had been built just before the Revolutionary War by ancestors on Henry Bradford's maternal side, and doubtless my mother's description would have fitted it then. But not since the 1800s had Bradhill, as it was now called, been a place for rumination, as opposed to meditation, or been "udderly" anything. The nearest Joyce's father had come to farming was the notion that he might raise swans, having the necessary pond and brook; but he soon heard swans were assertive, never forgot anything, and were frightened only by opened black umbrellas, and it all sounded too much like the sensitive people he had left in the city.

The house was on a hill, actually, and looked sweet and compact, though it was nothing of the sort. That was part of its charm; it looked so small and was so large, rambling as it did, wing after wing spread out, or neatly tucked in one upon another, like a very fat mother hen, giving no indication of her size until one is right up on the nest. As I say, I loved it; always had, since I first began to visit Joycie there, ages ago, for Easters, an occasional Christmas, and many weekends, when Mother was away, or couldn't have me at home for one reason or another.

The cheers that greeted our very belated approach floated out to us almost eerily as we went up the drive: we couldn't see them, but they knew we were coming. All the cousins were there, then, in full force, and their voices were high and joyful as they ran down the drive. I felt like a contestant in the Olympics, or at least the sister of one, as they stormed the car. Joyce was not first, and that was as it should be, and the cousin who kissed Bart, almost passionately and full on the mouth, was young and lush and someone he had never seen before. But her ardor was there; in honor, so perhaps even she believed, of the family. Joyce, languid, fluid as ever, came over quietly, waiting until her sister Lesley's soft shrieks had died down, and kissed Bart. He looked relieved, and returned her kiss as if he had been waiting for her with interminable restraint, then kissed her again, as if for good luck, as if he had won a bet on her. Then they curved together in an embrace that was all their own, very intimate, private, and kissed each other really for the first time. "You're late, you bridegroom you," she whispered.

"All Chloe's fault," he said, laughing, winking at me over his shoulder. "She had to stop for three martinis."

Joyce squeezed my hand. "I'm marrying a liar," she said.

"Anyway, we are still in time for the ceremony," I told her, but wondered why her hand felt so limp in mine.

She moved away quickly, detaching herself from me first, and then, rather hesitantly, from Bart.

"In just twenty-four hours!" cried the cousin whose name was Harriet and who was to be a flower girl, and joined with the others to drag Bart and Joycie, daisy-chain fashion, into the house.

I stood still by the car in the echo of laughter; I felt like a china doll, forgotten in the rain, and I watched the joyful cousins stalk forthrightly up to the house, slamming the screen door each in her turn as she went in the side entrance, as though it were a follow-the-leader game. When I went up the graveled drive they were all inside, except me. I stood for a moment and looked around, feeling the need again to think of quiet cool things. Joyce's house had never seemed this way to me before. I felt left out, forgotten—not unwelcome, but unthought of. And yet it had never seemed more beautiful, more my own. I felt as if I were looking at a place that was for sale and that I felt strongly inclined to buy. There was a sunset, there were hills, there was green everywhere. There was serenity, but in a minute, when I went inside as decorum obliged me to, there would be bedlam. A different kind from the bedlam of our house in town, but madness, incoherence, frustration…and this was my first wedding….

When I got inside they had all vanished, though I could hear the tantalizing echoes of concerted gaiety, somewhere in another wing of the house. I stood shocked for a moment by the weight of immediate silence which seemed to have nothing to do with the sounds of merriment that were now so far away.

Then I felt Joycie's arm around me. I would have known that arm anywhere. "Sweetie, cheer up. We're going to have a marvelous thing tonight—a real blast—after the rehearsal—"

I shook my head and turned away from her, tears blinding my eyes.

"Don't cry, baby doll. It doesn't matter that your mother couldn't come. You have to get detached from her sometime. Bart and I were saying that you—"

She broke off, and Ida Bradford, suddenly swooping down on us, enveloped me. "Darling," she crooned. "Joycie, go get her a Kleenex or something—darling, I know how *terrible* it is for your mother not to be able to come, but you *must* have a good time. Joycie and Bart will just hate it if you don't, and so will I."

I was ashamed of myself for crying and stopped at once and looked at her, even though I knew tears still clung in my lashes, and reddened my eyes. She smiled at me and held me back. "Why don't you go upstairs and wash that cute little face? Then slip into something to swim in. We're all going in the pool. Henry decided to fill it today."

"Today?" I marveled, for it was still chilly this early in the summer.

"Of course!" she said. "It's really just the time!"

She darted off, lithe as Joyce, more animated, younger-seeming even than the cousins. But I didn't go upstairs. I rather vaguely followed after her, to where she joined and put her arms about the waists of the younger butterfly cousins, young, young, young, younger than anybody in their light, bright summer dresses with the crinolines and full skirts. There were blue, green, pink, purple, and even black butterfly cousins flitting everywhere. They swarmed around, broke away, leaving two, one on either side, part of Queen Titania's entourage. Then they too were gone, probably to change into their swimming costumes, and she was left alone, hovering about—whispering to Bart, leaning over her husband, giving her daughter Lesley a little push toward the cousins. I stood at the window and gazed at them, and felt like a trespasser in a Disney forest. Then one of the servants opened the door which led to the side lawn, and their voices poured in, shrill, natural, sweet as birds—an aviary. I went upstairs to change.

Tennie had done most of my packing, and had chosen a very peculiar assortment of underthings and the dark pink swim suit I had meant to throw away. The rest of my clothes, thank Heavens, I had put out. I was glad that for once I would have a chance to unpack myself; I knew Gretchen and Loly were engaged in preparations for tomorrow and I would be completely undisturbed.

They had given me the room I almost always had, the one with the front view. I don't know whether I really preferred it or not, but I had had it so often that when I was given a different one occasionally, as at the time Joycie's French cousins were there and I came up for the weekend, I felt not just a mere visitor, but a transient. I was relieved this time to have my very own room again. Pleasure and well-being stole into me, even though I had not felt part of things downstairs, and because of this I decided to put on my swim suit in the bathroom, where there was a full-length mirror.

Even from there I could hear all the voices, and they somehow made me want to hurry. There were even splashing noises from the pool. I wriggled out of my clothes, feeling excited, eager, all of a sudden to get downstairs. I was glad it was a warm day because I knew the water would be terribly cold.

I had intended, I suppose, before anxiety set in, to stand in the bathroom before the mirror and look at myself, talk to myself, but now there wasn't time. I picked up the pink swim suit, giving only a look to me in the mirror, a look which I jubilantly told myself was a good look in every sense of the word, and squirmed and twisted the suit on. Then I stood there. No, I was not bad-looking. My hair, darker than when I was little, was thicker than my mother's, but I had my brother's nose. And though I was rather straight up and down, I wasn't disgustingly so. Not like I had thought I would be. I had hips, and breasts of a sort. Only I wasn't an hourglass. Not mature-looking. I must have sighed, because Joyce, when she came in the room, said, "Chloe, you look so sad, sweetie," and put her arms around me.

It surprised me and froze me to see her standing there beside me in the mirror. "You aren't going in the pool," was all I could think of to say to her, for she was there, fully clothed.

"If I do I'll look like a sea nymph tomorrow," she laughed, then went over and sat on the john. Then she got up, put up the lid and sat down again, having decided she really had to go.

"You'd better hurry up," she told me. "They've had it down there. Everyone's getting out."

"Who's everyone?" I asked.

"Oh, you, Chloe—" she laughed softly. "You always know, don't you? Just the cousins."

I shrugged, but the way she put it made the idea of joining the stragglers at the pool seem unattractive. She got up from the john. I loitered, adjusting a strap on my swimming suit, one I didn't need, really, since it was also meant to be strapless. "Chloe, does your mother hate me?" she said.

She said it when she was behind my back, though I could have been watching her in the mirror if I had thought she was going to say such a thing. I know I didn't gasp—I was watching myself—but I'm sure I looked surprised. I shook my head.

"She must hate me; must have always hated me even when she put up with me for all those nights I've spent at your house—your mother hates everybody." I shook my head, blindly, still looking at the mirror Joyce talking, not the real one. Her face seemed queerly distorted, asymmetrical. "Then why didn't she come? Why won't she come? Bart says she won't."

I turned and looked at her. "Joycie," I started, "how can I tell you—"

"Okay, don't," she said icily. "I know she thinks it's all a mistake and she wants no part of it. I know sense and reason are on her side and she feels it can't possibly work. Why don't you say that too? I'm sure you've thought it, that I'm like you, too young to fall in love and get married and everything. Why don't you be Miss Reason since your mother is obviously Mrs. Reason?"

She had left the room before I could answer, had slammed my bedroom door and gone off, as we used to say, in a Huffmobile. But this was serious; she was really angry, and more than angry, upset. I began to take off my swim suit; I knew I'd never make it to the pool now, and found myself slightly stunned. My hands seemed to be tingling, as if they had fallen fast asleep. Joycie was angry at me. Why? Because I was my mother's own child, the child of Reason. Reason!

Reason, I knew, lay snoring this minute on her bedroom chaise longue of striped green and white satin; still wearing, no doubt, the slightly soiled white hostess gown that Reason had worn into the den for coffee, for the *coup d'état*, the debate with Bart—the same hostess gown Kathleen had put out for the cleaners. All the more reason why Reason would tonight slightly vomit-stain the bright-green satin frogs which sometimes, as this morning, held the hostess gown shut; all the more reason why Reason would subsequently, after ten martinis, pass out and leave Jess to carry her to bed. Was I the child of Reason? Not this! Not this! I struggled into my clothes, eager to go after Joyce and have a talk with her—obviously Bart had failed.

As I thought of things to say, while I dressed, I tried to remember what she had said. How could I? I had been too stunned, too horrified. Then before I knew it, the whole lot of them were in my room, dancing around me like fireflies. Cousins everywhere, popping in one after another, like chain reactions, all urging me, pulling at me. "Come on, come on!" All of them ended this entreaty in a shriek of bliss, much more carefree than the principals of the wedding, I thought.

Then they bore me downstairs, captive, like a worm in a beak. Mrs. Bradford met me at the foot of the steps, by accident of course, but apparently she had already seen Joyce and knew all about it. "Never mind," she said, fondling my arm as if she loved it simply for its human warmth, "I'm sure she'll feel better tomorrow—then she's sure to come, so don't you worry, little pet. We'll have a fine time tonight and tomorrow she'll be here."

I shook my head, and was going to tell her why in a loud melodramatic explanation, but she had strayed, was now herding her thoughts, delivering them carefully to a man who had just come in and had met her as she went into the hall. These were all about his sleeping arrangements, but even from her tone I could tell she was preoccupied with them. Her voice, very fluent and persuasive, told whoever it was why he'd been given the attic to sleep in, that, yes, please do take up copies of *The New Yorker*, current and past, and she was so sorry, etc., that he had to be up there. Her face was wispy and glad—she was the Pollyanna "Glad Girl" type, despite her face with its careless frame of smoky disordered hair, her glamourous low-cut dress which no matter how recent the hour of attire reflected her wonderful figure in a slouchy way and appeared to have been put on backward. Mrs. Bradford was, for all this, a real beauty and would be so for years to come.

As she and the young man, whose face I couldn't see, went down the hall to the drawing room where the others were I could hear her little exclamatory vagaries answering, in their own way, whatever questions he was putting to her. Every inflection of her voice was predictable, as if she talked a sort of Palmer Method Penmanship speech, albeit a sloppy one; I always knew when she was going to say "darling."

She was still chatting to him when I came along the hall. "…We won't even think of the possibility of it not being a perfectly lovely day tomorrow…and tonight is sheer heaven, look at it. Shall we go watch them light the lanterns…?" But even while she was making these specific suggestions, her flowers, the vibrant cousins, were brushing her away and off with them to some far corner of nowhere.

I reached the drawing room door, expecting to find no one, for their voices now all sounded out-of-doors. But there he was, just as she had left him: Pritchard Allyn.

"I didn't know you were here," he said, and his voice was soft, relieved, yet very surprised.

I looked at him fleetingly; I couldn't trust myself longer, for his image was so much that of the Pritchard Allyn I had made up for myself that I couldn't bear, did not want, the original. "It's my brother Joyce is marrying, you know," I said, feeling quite strangled.

He gave me a quizzical look. I wondered if he, too, considered Bart an "old party"—some of the girls at school had called him that when they heard about the engagement. But what was Pritch doing here? "You are staying for the wedding," I heard myself say.

He nodded, his head, bright as ever, with its golden crown of hair. To think I had once touched it. Not once, but over and over again, in that corner of the hotel lounge behind the palms. "Yes, I'm down here with Tim Atkins. He's a friend of Joyce's too. And Lesley's," he added. "And his parents are friends of their parents, I think."

I looked at him again. This still did not explain him. Was

he anybody's friend? It was a funny time for a casual visit.

"Do you know Joyce or Lesley well?" I asked.

He nodded. "Lesley. Yes, I know her fairly well."

Jealousy is the color of green. It came up before my eyes as pure as if it had been squeezed out of a tube. So that was who he took to the prom he'd invited me to and never mentioned again; so that was why he hadn't answered my letters after that one dizzy meeting at the tea-dance. I turned away, maimed by a new misery. If Lesley had been going around with Pritchard Allyn, Joycie must have known. Why hadn't she told me? She knew how I'd fallen for him that afternoon. I wanted to sink into despair; my shoulders ached to slump. There was nothing but betrayal everywhere. I heard him move away, quietly. He had nothing to say to me, no apology to make. How could one apologize for having been taken seriously when the intention was frivolous? I was like a dullard who hadn't gotten the point of the joke.

"Dinner, dinner, dinner, everyone!" Ida Bradford was calling, and I saw people streaming from the back wing of the house toward the dining room—all the butterflies, and a certain number of young men, very correct and newly dressed and just arrived, apparently. The girls all had on their summer dresses, with sweaters lightly tossed over their shoulders, for they had been outside on the terrace, and they went in to dinner as they were. I looked at my own too-bouffant dress and hated it. Besides I wasn't hungry. But all the same I stood there watching them, at a distance, as they passed, and finally saw Bart and Joyce come in last. They looked chilled. And I thought to myself that they *should* look more chilled than the rest, for they were really warmer. What they had was so real, so warm, so lasting, that they were going to declare it legally, publicly. I shivered. Then I went in.

IV

The dining room was filled with small tables, set up to accommodate groups of four, and the double doors to the drawing room had been thrown back, and more tables had been set up there.

So far, only a sprinkling of people were wandering around the dining table on which dinner had been laid out, buffet style, and the others hung back, talking, laughing. There was a great wave of guffawing over by the sideboard where a bar had been temporarily established. The hard drinkers, some of Lesley's crowd, were there. I recognized, however, the Tim Atkins whom Pritchard had mentioned. Tim Atkins. He had written Joycie the awfulest letters last year. Crazy.

"I loathe cold salmon," Priscilla Maynard, a friend of Lesley's, said to me as she stepped up and tentatively took a plate.

"It's the cold salmon season," someone behind me remarked brightly. I looked around and it was Tim Atkins. "Hi," he said.

"Hi," I said, and started around the table too.

"Where are you sitting?" he asked. "How about in there?" He looked toward the drawing room. "All of the bridal party seems to be sitting in here, and all the parents and old stuff."

"All but one," said Priscilla with a laugh, and then her sweater fell from her shoulders.

"Are you old stuff or what?" Tim asked, picking up her sweater and laying it about her shoulders rather intimately. "My, my, my!" he exclaimed. "Look at all these precious jools!" he fondled the beadwork on her sweater, as if it were some particular part of her. She was pretty. She threw back her head and laughed at him, showing her perfect, almost tri-umphantly perfect teeth, and I thought to myself that she knew how to handle the smart ones, all kinds. She was eight-een, maybe nineteen. I knew some people who had sneaked into her deb party. "What do you put that silly streak in your hair for?" Tim asked her. Her hair was ash-blonde, but she had a snow-white artificial streak starting from her very envi-able widow's peak and going way back. My mother called it the "new skunk-do," whether the exhibitor had blonde hair or brown. And it wasn't so new. I too wondered why she did it.

Priscilla gave him another head-thrown-back laugh, also giving him a good view of the neck, the very long, slim, silken one; the skin fit her throat like a stocking.

"Which room are you in?" he asked, as he grabbed her elbow and gave it a suggestive squeeze. "Don't tell me. I might be tempted."

When she laughed again I decided that was all she knew how to do. But that was something. Admirably something.

"And how about you, Miss Whoever-you-are," he turned

to me. "Maybe I'll rape you tonight."

Priscilla shrieked at this, and he turned back to her. "You're safe," he told her. "They've got me above the garage. Not even in the guest house." And he didn't notice me after that.

I think I still felt rather funny when I sat down with them—why I did, I don't really know—and I wondered if I had been blushing. He, this Tim character, was awfully what my mother called *outré*. I knew he thought he was terribly funny. Maybe he even was, but he seemed young, inconsequential. Of course he hadn't remembered me, but then I'd only seen him twice, and met him only once. The one time, I think, Joycie had ever gone out with him. She had said he was awfully boring because he had kept talking all the way through the movie he took her to, all about how bored he was; how even his dreams bored him. I wondered, looking at him, all big eyes now for Priscilla, what made him so frantic. And I listened to him, too, for a while, as did the young man who had seated himself with us, a boy by the name of Andy Winthrop, also one of Lesley's crew.

Tim talked very fast, and used his head and hands a lot. He had a good head, and his very thick wavy dark hair kept curling down over his forehead when he gestured. He'd push it back and go on, or else he wouldn't push it back, and Priscilla would look as if she wanted to. He sounded rather witty too, but so awfully conceited that I merely smiled wanly instead of laughing because the conceit came through more than anything else.

Then Andy Winthrop broke in and began to tell a very

dull story, apropos of something so obscure that no one could trace its motivation, about Indian reservations. It seemed rather strange to hear him on such a primitive topic, for his voice was arch, sulky, as smooth as an old school tie. I knew he thought he was awfully good. He had what my mother describes as the "pear-shaped tones of the Burbank fruit," only I don't think he was a fairy; just talked that way. At times he looked scared.

I don't know why I noticed all of these things that night; the only reason I can give is that I was excited, if silent. Elation had taken the place of depression; I was accustomed to all that had happened, and had taken it, perhaps rightly, as the prelude to the brink of something. Certainly, I had no idea what. But my mind felt as if it were darting around and around, and I thought of a million things at the same time—miraculously, as I was able to sit there in apparent calm listening to these friends of Lesley's who were so pleased with themselves, so witty and smart. So sophisticated. Of course I would have preferred sitting with Joycie, talking, but that was clearly out of the question, and somehow, sitting where I was, I felt terribly alive and alert, giddy, free. Then, too, I had lots of wine. Tim kept filling my glass; he always noticed when it was empty, even though he didn't once notice me. And I wasn't used to wine. We almost never had it at home because Mother always concentrated so hard on the martinis that she couldn't be bothered, and of course when I was with Aunt Maude I'd been much too young.

As I drank it, I watched Tim, safely, over the rim of my glass. He fascinated me, even if his chin was too weak and his hair too lustrous. But he had wonderful eyes. Very expressive, luminous, like those one would imagine a foreign count having. They were love eyes; Latin eyes. They were sort of grown-up eyes, too. I'd never looked into any quite like them level-to-level, with a right to, that is. But his certainly did not look back into mine. Not then.

I think they began to when I suddenly remembered, out loud, the time I had first met Priscilla. Years ago. She and her mother and grandmother had come to tea at the Bradfords, and her grandmother had told us a fascinating story about how she had crossed from England on a small steamer once when she was a young woman and they had run into an iceberg.

"How on earth could you remember that after all this time?" Priscilla exclaimed at me, pushing back her hair.

"Was there anything particularly memorable about it?" asked Andy in his affected voice, which now also sounded rather sneering.

Then Priscilla told them the iceberg story. "It seems they ran into an iceberg and part of it broke off and fell on deck," Priscilla said.

"Do tell," said Andy, very bored.

"—And there was a polar bear encased in the ice and the rest of the passengers—"

"You mean the polar bear was a passenger—?" Tim put in.

"No, silly ass," she laughed. "I mean the *passengers* all got together and pushed it off the deck."

"Anybody they knew?" asked Tim.

"Where were the stewards?" asked Andy.

"Oh, well," Priscilla dilated her eyes at them and smiled. The story had certainly fallen flat. Somehow it occurred to me that they thought it was my fault. They didn't say anything; didn't even look at me, but there was a heaviness of feeling in the air, the accusing feeling of responsibility.

Now they just ate, looking at each other from time to time. Finally, Tim said, "An amusing little story, rather."

"Yes." Andy gave a drawling echo.

"But what did it mean? I mean *mean*? What message did it have for me?" Tim asked in an innocent sly voice, obviously out to trap somebody.

"Yes, tell us, Priscilla," Andy put in. "Is the moral 'stay away from wild animals on tramp steamers'?" He almost yawned with satisfaction over this quip, as if he felt he could retire on it.

"No. It meant 'Fly Air France,'" I told him, hardly believing my ears as I said it. How had I dared open my mouth!

"Eeeeeeeee!" Tim leaned over, breaking up, so pleased he was with this rejoinder.

I stared at him rather dazed. Then he screamed and choked and then Priscilla pounded him on the back. "It wasn't that funny," I said, and noticed that Andy's face indicated he couldn't have agreed with me more. He was one of those who didn't like it when someone else said something funny.

"Was! Was!" Tim assured him so loudly that lots of other people turned around. "Funny girl, very funny girl! What's your funny name, funny girl?"

"Oh, Tim," Priscilla remonstrated with a protectiveness that was like a knife in my chest and a shield before her own.

"Funny Chloe Longtree," I told him.

"Little ole Chloe? Bart's teenie tiny sister?" he gasped, still laughing, though both Priscilla and Andy looked somber; indeed Andy looked petulant and bored.

"I know you," I said slowly, meaningfully, and returned to my food.

This brought a howl of spiteful pleasure from both Priscilla and Andy, but Tim was undaunted. "You certainly are Cornelia's daughter!" he said, and baffled though I was over how he had ever come to have the audacity to call my mother by her first name, I didn't turn a hair, move one, or answer him. I just kept on eating.

Then he said lots of things, leaning on his elbow, looking directly at me, I knew, though I didn't once stop eating to look up at him. He was more or less wooing me.

He kept saying semi-insulting things, along with clever ones, or ones he thought were clever, like, "Say, sweetie, you're not half bad. What made me think you were a dumb blonde? Has old Joycie been poisoning your tiny Chinese mind against me? Is that why you won't look at me? Look at me! I like you. You're great." Finally he said, "Are you bombed, is that why you won't answer?" and that was too much.

"No," I told him. "I'm stoned. Stoned to death. Somebody ought to tell you about lethal weapons. They're not as funny as they look."

Priscilla and Andy just howled.

"I'm ape for you," he told me then, quietly, almost endearingly, but by that time I felt numb and scared.

Yet, when we got up from the table I realized I felt more than that. I felt pleased with myself, mentally regal, and now that I look back on it, rather dizzy with elation. Vaguely I knew I had scored on an upper level. Priscilla and Andy and Tim were older; they almost belonged to the grown-up world, the one over the horizon, only these people I could still touch. I felt tired but ecstatic, as if I had stretched myself.

"What means 'ape,' Atkins?" I heard Priscilla ask Tim. They were behind me. I was floating along, out of the drawing room, a little tipsy.

"You'll never know," he told her.

But being 'ape' when Priscilla wasn't can never make up for what was to follow. Joycie caught up with me. Bart wasn't there.

"Talk to you," she murmured and steered me rather hurriedly toward the stairs. We started up together and Joycie was whispering, her voice very earnest, but so low I couldn't understand her, when Lesley caught up with us. "Where's the dress?" she asked.

Joycie shook her head. "Ask Mother," she said.

"But Priscilla has to have it now!" Lesley insisted.

"Ask Mother, damn it!"

"Oh, you idiot!" Lesley said with deep scorn. "I wish to God all this was over with!"

"So do I!" Joyce blazed back at her. "And just you wait— if you ever get married—!"

"Go to hell," Lesley said and bounded back down the

stairs.

I looked at Joyce. "Wait till we get to my room. Then I'll tell you," she said.

It struck me as rather odd that she didn't really seem to mind what Lesley had said, which was not like her; she just kept on going up the steps, very rapidly, purposefully. She and Lesley had had a terrible sibling thing; had scratched and bitten each other. This wasn't like Joyce. It was something awfully serious then.

I followed along, stumbling a little. I wanted to hum to myself. I still felt light-headed, but I didn't hum. Besides, there would be lots of champagne later. And there would be Tim—this I was sure of. Maybe there would even be Pritchard. I had changed. I had changed!

I was on the point of telling Joycie I had changed, and how much, all about it, when she quietly closed the door to her room behind us. "Priscilla didn't tell you?" she asked, her hands still on the door.

"Tell me what?" I sank down on the edge of her bed. Same old Joycie. Same old room. Over in the corner was the life-size stuffed toy lion named "Petit Lion" after a real one in a book by the same name my mother had given her on her ninth birthday. And there was the ten-gallon hat hung on the wall beside the Noh mask her dead brother had sent her from Japan. Nothing changed.

"I've got to tell you," said Joyce, almost sounding frightened. "I have to, but I'm awfully glad Priscilla didn't get around to it—I thought absolutely that she would, the bitch—"

"What?" I asked. Joyce looked so miserable.

"Oh, Chloe!" she shook her head. "What an awful day!"

I stared at her.

"It is! It is!" she insisted. "It isn't mine at all! Everything's so cruddy and distressful."

This is an act, came looming into my mind like a movie title in a foreign film, explaining everything. I sat up sharp and throbbing now, because indeed I knew it was awful. Especially if she said so like that.

"What's happened? Did Mother call up and say she was coming to stop the wedding?"

"She did call, as a matter of fact," Joycie said to me in surprise. "How did you know that?"

"Is she coming?" I asked, equally surprised to have guessed something like that.

"No, no," Joyce shook her head unhappily again. "She just called. But so did my cousin Nance Ramsey. She can't come either." She looked at me imploringly, her eyes hanging on mine.

"She was to have been a bridesmaid," I said.

Joyce nodded. I waited, but nothing came.

I looked down at my new shoes. I pointed one toe at nothing. Then the other one. I couldn't quite bear to speak, although I knew I was expected to; knew if I didn't that no one would. Ever. "What did Bart say?" I finally asked her, but I couldn't look at her.

"He said you'd never forgive me," Joyce answered. She was really crying now and she sounded as if she would choke.

For what? For what? For what? The thought screamed in

my mind. But I couldn't ask her. "I see," I said, and I felt stiff as I got up from her bed and started toward the door. I felt slow and circumlocutory, but it had to be that way. In any event I couldn't go near her. If she would only get away from that door. Then I could just walk out.

"Where are you going?" she cried, in a voice just short of a scream. She was really scared now. "Alarmed" was the gentlest, most euphemistic word that could have been summoned to describe the look on her face. But I didn't really look at it; couldn't; it made me ill. What a friend. "I suppose the dress fitted Priscilla perfectly, Nance's dress?"

"Oh, Chloe, you *don't* understand!" she rebuked me.

I looked at her then, thoroughly hating her. I remembered all the times at school—all the excuses she made for fixing other people up with the extra men her dates brought along, all the weekends I'd been asked to that were suddenly canceled, all the times I'd done her Soc Sci work for her in the library, the papers she had copied, the toys she had borrowed and never returned. "Yes, I do," I told her almost cheerfully. "It goes like this: Your cousin Nance wrenched her left tendon, or whatever it was she was always dislocating when she played tennis, and couldn't come to wear that great big dress, and Priscilla was the same size, which I'm not—"

"But I *wanted* you, Chloe! I did! I did!"

"—and your sister Lesley decided it was a good idea to have her friend Priscilla Maynard take her place because after all Priscilla is very, very popular and might get married any one of these days and then she'd have to ask Lesley.—Isn't that it?" I leveled a look at her.

"No, sweetie, Chloe! Chloe! I couldn't help it!"

"No doubt," I said. "After all, you're only getting married, but a wedding is everybody's affair. Anyway," I paused and looked back at her from the door. "Thanks. Thanks for thinking of me. I'll be a bridesmaid yet, just you see."

After that, I went down the stairs. They were like a waterfall I descended, a cascade of my tears.

V

"Mole, Mole, Mole," Bart said over and over, and put his arms around me—really restraining me, because I know he knew I was intent on going home. I would have done it too, if he hadn't said the one false consolation in the world: "Cry," he said; "you'll feel better." He hadn't even noticed I *was* crying!

After that everything seemed to dry up; soft things hardened. I hated his false sympathy; knew he didn't feel it, and all my tears dried, as naturally as a spent geyser. I can't describe how I felt, but it was wanton, cruel. I longed for Joyce to appear so I could do something really awful to her and laugh about it. I could have too, just then.

But everyone was ready for the rehearsal, except Joyce. I went into the drawing room and there everyone was, and a lot of other people besides, drinking champagne. The rector, a very, very old man, staggered from side to side, and laughed as if he hadn't gotten the point. Then someone told me he had been sleeping one off in the library and they had just waked him up. I felt sorry for him. But still no Joyce.

The lights were on outside. Electric spotlights, as the Japanese lanterns were now very dim. From time to time the cousins darted outside experimentally and came back shivering in their sweaters. It really was going to be too chilly tomorrow for an outdoor wedding; everyone knew it, but everyone was very happy on champagne.

I don't know when Joyce came down, but it was awfully late, and everyone trooped out to the garden in a great hurry to have the outside part over with and come back for more champagne.

I'm sure I was one of the last ones out on the lawn, and I watched the proceedings dully, through a glass very darkly, for I had had more champagne than I'd ever had in my life, was very sad, and very deserted. Inside, I had talked to Bart's best man, who had finally arrived from Boston, and he had twitted me about being a "little speck of a creature" when he and Bart had been roommates at Harvard; and I had talked to some of the ushers, and once had even been beside Pritchard. No more Tim. And now there was nobody, and it was cold.

The wedding music, supplied by the piano inside, came out to us as if broadcast from the frozen North. The accompanist, who would play tomorrow, was high as a kite, and at the distinct disadvantage of being inside, not able to tell how things were going.

I don't know why I slipped off, but I did. I felt as I had years before, as a real child, during Mother's parties. Somehow the hilarity was not for me. I wanted to be alone.

Inside, I sneaked by the half-drunk pianist, grinning to herself with spirit and determination as she banged out her wedding music, and crept down the steps to the hall. Once past her, I knew there was no one else in the house, nothing to detect me and send me back, but I used stealth. The truth was that I felt raw, like an exposed nerve, throbbing. I didn't even want the walls to know I was there.

So I crept along, passing from room to room in the darkened, quiet house. How many rooms there were, I realized painfully, and such little ones, stingy, low-ceilinged, pinched together like the portraits—oddly hostile—of ancestors who adorned the walls. These little rooms! How many more? Built so they would retain the heat, the early American heat, so hard to come by, so carefully garnered, so thriftily watched through the icy blasts of bygone winters. I opened the latched door into another room. It was a witch door. The panels built in the shape of a cross, to keep witches out, so it was said. Who had told me that? Where had I learned it? Daddy would have known. Daddy, Daddy! I think I sobbed this aloud at one point, then I went on. I knew then that I wanted to get to a telephone, one somewhere I could talk, so I could call Mother.

I counted the fireplaces. Only three more, then I would be in the room in the end wing where Joycie and I used to watch TV when they had first moved up here; when TV—which they had called Television—had been new. I not only counted the fireplaces, I counted the steps I had to go up to get down to another room; then the steps down. Then there was the passageway, off to one side. I would creep down this, as if it were a labyrinth in a cave, and thus avoid the new part of the house, the "modern" part where all the furniture was different and strange, cold as a price tag. I turned into the little hall as if it were my own secret passage; it joined the old house with the new, but I would not have to see the new. The little room had a telephone, a fireplace, chintz-covered furniture. It also had, I discovered, Tim Atkins. He was asleep on the couch. Apparently he hadn't made it to his room over the garage or hadn't wanted to.

I suppose I backed out into the passage again when I saw him there. I can remember watching the top of his head. It didn't move, of course, because he was asleep. It looked intrusive, first of all, however handsome and sleek. He was to me an enemy sentinel, taken unawares.

I went right past him, stormed over to the telephone and put a call in to my mother in New York. Tim Atkins heard me talking to the operator, woke up and blinked at me stupidly. I could have killed him. "Hello," he said softly, with an insinuating intonation. I didn't look at him. Maddeningly, I heard the phone ring time after time. Why didn't someone answer?

He was sitting up on the couch now, his arm stretched along the back of it, watching me, alert, waiting. I pretended I still thought I was going to get an answer, though I knew I wasn't.

"Why don't you hang up?" he asked me finally. And just because he said this I let it ring a little while longer. Until the operator, that diehard, told me at last that the number didn't answer and she'd be glad to try in twenty minutes.

I put down the phone, and he took my hand. "Were you calling your mama?" he asked gently.

I know I must have looked as if I could have killed him,

but he only tightened his hold on my hand. "You're such a little girl," he said, and drew me down beside him.

I got up immediately. But he pulled me down. "They won't be in here for hours—if ever," he said. I looked at him and hated his eyes, his eyes that I had found so fascinating before.

"Let me go," I said.

"You want to go to Pritchard?" he asked.

This room…I freed my hand, tried to get up. Nothing seemed safe. This old, cozy room seemed alien, turned against me, and there he was, holding my hand, looking at me that way.

"Look," I said, "I don't know…I don't know…but I want to be by myself…"

"You almost are…"

I know I violently shook my head at that. "Let me go," I said. "I want to."

Then he kissed me.

I hardly know how to describe it; I know I didn't like it, but it was something very soft, very strange, very compelling. I remember I opened my eyes and looked at him. Looked in his eyes. They were covered over with a kind of a film, full of some totality I still can't explain. It was, of course, desire, but it was something else; something like "all." "I'm falling in love with you," he said.

I shook my head, but he nodded his, reached for my mouth, and there he was kissing me again. "I want to make out with you," he said, "even though I know you are a virgin. I'll take the consequences. I'll even marry you."

Then I got up, though he was trying to hold me down. I stood up, even though his arms were around my legs. My heart was going like a racing car, careening around corners, throbbing in my temples. "I've got to go," I know I said.

"Not yet, not yet. You're so wild….Lie down beside me."

Why did I ever do it? But I did. I lay down beside him until dawn. It came in the windows, beyond the chintz curtains, over the gardens, across the bower built for the wedding. And there we lay, Tim and I, together.

I think we both must have slept; I don't know. But I do know that whatever it was, we were together. I didn't care, lying there with him, whether I ever saw anybody else again. I suppose I could say it was the champagne, but it wasn't. And nothing really happened. We were just together. His arms around me; mine around him. And every time I moved he kissed me. Then I kissed him. And we were there together. "Angel, darling, wild angel, darling," I'll never forget how he said that. Over and over.

PART TWO

I

"Man, oh man, oh Manischewitz!" Portia exclaimed, her eyes bugging out the way they do when she's excited. She was sitting cross-legged on her bed, rolling up her rather greasy hair. It was the color of a wet sidewalk, really needed a bath, not just a curl. "Then what happened? If that's not the livin' end," she shook her head again in emphasis, thinking about what I'd just said. I was telling her about the wedding.

"Then he started on the baptismal ceremony again," I went on.

"Again?" Portia cried, her eyes looking more buggy than ever behind the heavy glasses. She was so ugly that sometimes she made me uncomfortable, so I looked away as I went on telling her about it.

It was funny, uproarious in fact. I enjoyed it all over again. Portia was about the ninth person I'd told it to because I hadn't seen her when I came in the night before or all day either. She had been asleep when I got back to school, was still in those heavy, rusty-looking flannel pajamas, probably burning up with the heat. I'd turned on the light just for a moment, and she had stirred, frowned a little, her face all scrubbed and pink, looking troubled like a baby's, and bitten up by mosquitoes, only the bites in her case were pimples. Portia was having a hard time with adolescence. She was only fifteen and so unattractive you wanted to cry for her. She'd never been out with a boy in her life and was, of course, simply man-mad. But she was awfully smart. Terribly brilliant, particularly in math. I liked old Portia; somehow I enjoyed telling her about the wedding more than I had telling anyone else. She was so excited, reacted so well. Only I couldn't tell her all of it…couldn't possibly…not about Timmy.

I guess I must have fallen silent, as I lay there, my arms behind my head, because she said, "Well, go on, go on…didn't the old frost ever get the right lines?"

The "old frost" was the rector who had married Bart and Joycie on Saturday, the one who had gotten so spiffed the night before at the rehearsal party. I don't know whether it was a hangover, old age or what, but halfway through the ceremony—and God, it had been cold out there, like the first day of March instead of June—he had trailed off into nothing, or rather just a mumble, and when he cleared his throat and recovered himself, much to everyone's astonishment he was doing the baptismal service.

"Go on, go on!" Portia urged me again, jumping up and down with impatience. "Did they ever get married or just baptized?"

"Oh, they finally got married," I said rather dreamily, for my mind had moved on again, and I was thinking of Tim. Maybe I could tell her about Tim. "You know those Chagall wedding paintings?" I asked her.

"Tell me again how Joycie looked," Portia said not bothering to take any notice of my question. "Was she really shivering?"

"Certainly she was. All of them were," I told her.

"Boy, what a shame! Gee," Portia commented.

"They didn't seem to mind."

"Still it was a shame."

"Umm," I murmured.

"Was that all? How about the reception? What happened there?"

"The usual," I said making my voice sound sleepy. She rather irritated me. Besides I wanted to think. I rolled over, face down on my bed, then I turned my head toward the wall. I heard her sigh.

"You want me to put out the light?" she asked in a low voice.

I purposely did not answer, though my eyes were wide open. I couldn't have slept if I had to, but I didn't want to talk any more. It was only about ten-thirty, a half-hour until lights out, but maybe she would think I was dead tired. I was, in fact. But I fairly hummed inside with alertness. The whole thing was passing through my mind, vivid, acutely alive, the agony and ecstasy; it would slow down then speed up, then slow down again. I couldn't control it, I could only watch.

Even this much later, I have trouble remembering it sensibly, and now, of course, it is fragmentary too—whole patches are missing. It's a sort of moth-eaten tapestry at this point. But what remains is vibrantly, shimmeringly real. Particularly the pain of it. But that night in our room, I was sensitive to the rest of it too. It was so very wonderful. It made me shiver, it was so wonderful. And I never see those Chagall wedding paintings—whether at the Modern, or just reproductions—without feeling that shiver of ecstasy again, as if I had witnessed a miracle.

The day of Joycie's wedding I was like the Chagall bride; I was floating in the air, a bridal bouquet in my hands. Only my hand was in Timmy's. We stood very far at the back, together, the recipients of all sorts of long, meaningful looks from everyone from Joyce's mother to Bart. I think they all knew what we were up to, but everyone was too harassed by the wedding business to stop and bother with me. But of course no one knew how it had started. No one knew that I had stayed with Timmy until dawn in the back sitting room. No one knew that I even knew him very well. They must have been very puzzled.

It was a very pretty wedding, and the sun was out, though it was cold as an icicle. I had on an old spring coat of Joyce's, and nearly everyone there except the bridal party was all wrapped up and snug. And if that old imbecile hadn't forgotten the marriage ceremony, it wouldn't have been so bad. Everyone was giggling by the time he actually got back on it, and lots of women, especially in the back near us, were whispering about it. "Shocking!" "She should have known better than to have *him*. Everyone knows his mind's gone." "—all because he married her and Henry—"

Timmy pinched my finger when it was all over. "Roger!" he exhaled a sigh. "I thought they'd never make it. That's the last lesson I'll ever need about sentimental indulgences.

Nothing like that is going to happen to us, is it?"

I just melted away.

This was the part I was thinking of that night, that last night of school, there with Portia. This was the part that always came back to me after that, clearer than anything else. I lay there musing about it, going over and over it in my mind. Then the beginning would flash by again, stop, speed up, slow down. The parts about Joyce and Bart caught on a snag, but I wasn't angry at them any more, or hurt or anything. I simply didn't care. For them I felt cold; for Timmy I felt warm.

When I heard Portia switch off the light, I moved slightly, sort of twitched my finger experimentally, for I had been lying there rigid as a sarcophagus so she wouldn't bother me. Then when I heard the slight click the frames of her glasses made as she put them down on the table beside her bed, I jumped up, darted around past her bed and had my hand on the door before she sat up and said, "I thought you were asleep, you faker!" Her voice was more startled, actually, than accusing.

"I'm not," I said hurriedly. "'Bye," and I shut the door behind me as I went out in the hall.

The first person I met was "Dusty" Rhodes, the hall monitor. Dusty was a swell all-around guy. "Lights out in ten minutes," she said genially, and gave me a wink. I knew she would report me if I didn't make it back, but I knew she wouldn't want to. Anyway, it didn't matter. Maybe I wouldn't be coming back next fall either, so they could have their silly demerits and call-downs. My heart leaped up at the thought, agile, prancing, like a pet terrier. But joy stopped as I passed Joyce's door. I wouldn't be stopping there tonight. Or ever again. She was gone. She and Bart had flown off on Saturday. No one knew where they were going, only Mother thought it might be Capri. She had a feeling Aunt Maude had let them have her house there.

Avery Stafford's room was on the third—my destination. "Come!" she called out when I knocked. I still always knocked at her door, for I didn't know her that well, really.

Mary Barkley was sitting on Avery's bed. They both looked around at me as if I had interrupted something, only Avery looked as if she didn't mind. "Ta," said Mary, standing up.

She was wearing a transparent peignoir over a pair of very much too shorty-pajamas. Her legs looked unnaturally long and brown. Mary was a good hockey player. She was much taller than Avery or I, rather stately, and because she was dark, one of those rosy-skinned glowing brunettes, she looked older than she was, sort of worldly and wise. But she was dumb as hell. Couldn't even begin to compete with Portia for brains. I know she didn't like me; she always connected me somehow with Portia, thought we crewed around together, was surprised when she heard Joyce was going to marry my brother, that we had all known each other for centuries. But then she never noticed anything. She was very absorbed in herself.

"Don't go," Avery told her, but didn't sound as if she meant it.

Mary shook her head, gave me a rather abbreviated nod,

and went out.

"Who stepped on her tail?" I asked.

"God," said Avery. "He did it first, then everybody else followed. That girl is riddled with paranoia."

"She is?" I asked incredulously. Mary had always seemed to me the heart and sweet breath of self-possession, hateful though I found her personally.

"You should hear the way she was carrying on. Said nobody in school liked her; how Joycie didn't even ask her to her wedding."

"Why should she have?" I asked, finding it all passing strange.

"Oh, she considered Joycie her best friend."

"Why? Just because she went up there once or twice for a weekend? Joyce always told me the reason Mary came was because she more or less invited herself and Joycie couldn't think of a way out of it. Anyway, you know she couldn't have gone. Joycie would have asked lots of people if they could have gotten off from school." I didn't look at Avery as I said this, for I was telling the tiniest faintest white lie: Joycie wouldn't have invited Avery, school or no school. I knew this, but I felt sorry for Avery. Maybe she was sort of psycho, but she had reason to be. And anyway she had a terrific sense of humor and was always tearing around to all sorts of places on the weekends, living it up whenever she got the slightest opportunity. Her specialty was Yalies. I didn't even know any. Joycie considered her a J.D., dismissed her.

"What was all that you were telling me about Tim Atkins last night when you came in? You made sense none."

Actually, this was what I had come to talk to her about, for last night she had said, "Oh, I know *him*," when I casually mentioned that he was more or less my date at Joycie's, and now I wanted to find out why she had said it so meaningfully. "Brief me," I answered her. "I don't remember what I said either."

Avery laughed. Her laughter was one of the best things about her. It really did sound as if it came from a bell, it was always silver, and sometimes it pealed, sometimes just tinkled. It was wonderful. "You must have been bombed or something when you came in," she gave me an amused look.

"A little gone anyway," I confessed. But it hadn't been from drinking, for actually I had simply come straight to school from home. Of course Timmy had driven me down from Connecticut, on Sunday, but he had to go back to Cambridge first thing the next morning because his car was in the garage there or something and he had rented that one for the weekend, so he wanted to turn in early. He was staying with his cousins, he had said, down on Gramercy Park. I didn't know them.

"Timmy's something of a bad actor. But I guess you noticed," Avery told me. "He'll even drink perfume."

I was faintly surprised, but I knew this was just defensiveness. Actually, four days ago I would have agreed with her. Until the second time, I met him, that is. Reluctantly, I was rather sure she was right and decided to listen. Only I knew that right or not, eventually she would change her mind, for Tim Atkins would change. In fact, being perfectly objective as I sat there and thought about it, I decided he had already begun to change, but of course this was nothing to say to Avery.

"How long have you known him?" I asked, deliberately saying it in an offhand way. But though it sounded casual to me, I wondered, for Avery was nothing if not discerning.

"Moons and moons," she told me. "Or I might say until he stopped knowing me particularly."

"Oh?" I said with polite interest.

"Yes, sweetie, that one is a *bad* bad actor, a great dropper of hot cakes."

I supposed she was deliberately being mysterious, so it wouldn't do to press her, but I could feel my blood plunging around in my veins. I was sort of furious at her, but more, I had a sinking feeling that she was thinking something very awful, maybe too awful to say. But still I had to know.

Avery gave me a cool appraising look, saw that I wasn't going to commit myself one way or the other. "How old are you, Chloe? Are you younger than Joyce, or where did I get that idea?"

Somehow she made me feel as if I'd be indicting myself if I told her the truth, but I had to be straight-arrow with her because I wanted her to be with me. Anyway she always was. She was that way. She would even be about Timmy, even if she got a glimmer of how important it was to me. If it was terrible she wouldn't hold back—I'd just get it on the line. "I'm going to be seventeen," I told her.

Again I got her silver laughter. "Well, then, you're safe for a couple of years. Or one at least." I raised my eyebrows. "Oh, sweetie, Timmy's not a boy wonder, you know. He's a

Papageno, a birdman." I still looked puzzled. "A nest featherer!" she exclaimed. "Timmy hasn't got a bean, but he knows a feather when he sees one."

"Strike two," I said with a short kind of gulping laugh that I immediately wished I had somehow suppressed. "I'm too young for the course and I haven't any sweepstakes to offer."

"Don't give me that," Avery said. "Your mother is bent double with the burden of her jack—everybody knows that."

"But I'm not. Never will be. My mother prides herself on being an heirless heiress. She promises me 'comfort,' that's all."

Avery viewed me quizzically, and I knew she was tempted both not to believe me and to explore. I was glad she didn't because it was humiliating to have to try to explain. Anyway, I couldn't have. My mother's fixations, or "ideas," as she called them, about money had always escaped me. Sometimes it even occurred to nee that maybe she didn't really have any to speak of, just wanted people to think so. Or maybe she really did and planned to make me an heiress, but just didn't want to spoil me now. Anyway, I was certainly thoroughly "disciplined" about the importance of money, though she wasn't herself.

"There's the bell," I said and started to get up.

"Stick," Avery said. "They won't cheek for another ten minutes."

"Rhodes will," I told her at the door, and gave her a glum smile since that was the only kind I had to offer. "She saw me come np."

Avery pushed the hair out of her eyes. It was fluffy and blonde—almost albino. "Mothers are rascals, aren't they?" she said.

I nodded and went out. My eyes blurred with tears; they had come on without my noticing, like a summer shower. Yet they were sadder than summer ever could be. They were winter rain. What she had said—about Timmy, about Mother—was serious. They had both gotten the axe. And they both deserved it.

II

Avery graduated that year, a year behind. I sat in the Junior section, up front, two days later at Commencement, and looked at her in her white gown and mortar board. She was all white. A sort of Easter lily. Even her eyebrows.

A very noted somebody addressed us, or the graduating class, and told them all the usual. Having heard it for three years, I certainly felt no need to listen. Anyway, in my pocket I had two special deliveries from Tim, and a telegram from my mother. I had plenty to think about. Tim was coming down and she was going up. He was coming down from Cambridge, where he was a graduate student, and Mother was flying to Capri—to prey on Bart and Joycie. She said she had tried to telephone me at school, but she hadn't. If I hurried after this bit was over, I might be able to drive out to the airport with her. Then back just in time to meet Tim for tea. "At the Plaza at four. Palm Court. It's a date (no puns please)." I had giggled hysterically when I read his letter that morning, but then her wire had arrived. This certainly did something to summer plans. What now? What was I supposed to do? We had a house in Glen Cove, but *I* couldn't open it up. We hadn't been out for three straight summers now. She always found something else to do. Thank God this time I was too old to be sent to camp. "Camp Laughing Willow." The mere thought of the place destroyed me.

I looked at Avery again, and she caught my eye. She fluttered one lid, illustrating her exhaustion. I knew she hadn't had any sleep the night before—nor had I for that matter. For the last two nights we had sat up after lights talking. I had told her the whole thing with Timmy, and she had filled me in on him. All she knew. I had a case history of his whole deb-chasing career, even knew about the bit he had had with Mary Barkley last summer at Montauk when their sailboat was supposed to have capsized. And nobody knew that except Avery. Avery seemed to know everything. It was hard for me to believe that I had known her all these years and hadn't known her at all. Of course Avery was a sad case and she made a point of having it solo. And other people made a point of letting her have it that way, for her name wasn't even mud.

Avery's mother, for whom she was named, had been blessedly killed in an accident about three years before. And it was always put that way when people spoke of it. A real bated-breath subject, for she had been *the* Avery Cowles, a big smash hit in the late thirties, known as "the toast of West Point" and, as somebody had added, "the meat and potatoes of the entire Ivy League." She was a wild one. And Avery's grandmother was afraid Avery was going to be just like her. Well, she was.

Avery lived with her grandmother, "quietly," as Avery put it, in Southampton. In the winter Mrs. Cowles went to

Taormina and Avery went to Chalmers. She had been going ever since I had, I know, and probably before. Now, like Joyce, she wouldn't be going any more. I wondered what would happen to her. I know she didn't think much of the idea of going on with the mind-improving routine. She wasn't going to be any Smith College Woman, if she could help it. But I knew she wasn't planning to come out either. What could happen to her? I felt genuinely concerned. I had grown very fond of Avery. Something good had to happen to her. It just had to. She'd had enough rough things. I wondered what her grandmother was like. I hadn't a clue. Of course Mother probably had it all at the top of her tongue, but I had never thought to ask before, because then I hadn't cared; hadn't thought much about Avery one way or the other.

I was sitting beside Portia, and just then I felt her nudge me. She gestured toward the entrance of the auditorium. "Dig that," she said.

"Dig what?" I whispered back. I couldn't see anything.

She shook her head. "Gone now," and then she looked straight ahead of her, with the innocent concentrated stare that she wore in class, the one that made the others think she was so pathetic, so guileless. Open that head, I thought, and you'll find the entire male locker-room population all running around in their all-togethers without so much as a towel. For this reason, I looked again toward the entrance, for I was pretty sure that she must have spotted masculine flesh. But there was nobody.

I felt the letters in my uniform pocket, and that damned

telegram. Would this thing never cease? How much could the human ear endure? I was all packed. All I had to do was go by the room that Joycie had had and get her tennis racket and a box out of the top of her closet—. Portia nudged me again. "Look! Look!"

There in the doorway, peeking in, was Pritchard Allyn. I stared at him.

"Maybe Chalmers is going co-ed," Portia giggled, but I still hadn't recovered. What *was* he doing here? Portia must have gathered that I knew him. "Name please? Telephone number?" She giggled so loudly, squawked really, that several people turned around, including the chapel proctor. But she couldn't hurt us now.

Pritchard was looking over the heads of the crowd, searching for someone. Just then Timmy joined him, and it was all I could do to keep from leaping up. Portia hadn't missed a trick. "Yours, I might have known," she said in mock sadness, hardly bothering to lower her voice.

Somehow I managed to get their attention, and they waved and gestured. Then they made faces and threw their arms around sending semaphore conveying that they would wait outside the chapel.

Desperately, I took stock of the situation. The diplomas hadn't even been handed out yet. At least another thirty minutes. And what was I going to do anyway? I *had* to see Mother. I rattled the telegram in my pocket, fished it out and read it again. The plane left at two, just as I thought. That meant she had to leave as near one o'clock as possible.

I knew Portia was watching every move I made, absolutely consumed with curiosity. Poor old Portia. "Can I meet them?" she whispered.

I nodded. There was nothing else to do; if I had shaken my head she would have had a stroke. Anyway, maybe there would be time. And Avery—I crumpled the telegram up and jammed it back in my pocket, making another terrific noise, and began to chew on the inside of my mouth. I do that whenever I'm nervous. Usually people ask me if I have a toothache, but of course Portia was used to it; she was my roommate. Still, I reminded myself, I'd have to stop it. I was discouraged from this nervous diversion by one and by all, particularly by Miss Fleming who was our hall hostess, and she was sitting in the first seat in the next aisle. Oh, hell, I thought, what do I care? Anyway, I was more sure than ever I'd never see old Chalmers again, not from the inside looking out. I glanced nervously toward the entrance, but Timmy and Pritchard had disappeared. What was Pritchard doing here? Of course they knew each other from Harvard; even though Pritch was an under-graduate, they were friends and all, and I supposed it was natural enough that they had come down together. Still—. And I bit the inside of my cheek again, gave it a good gnaw. Then I stopped. Was I nervous because Pritchard was here? Ho, ho. What a thought!

I looked back again at the row of sweet girl graduates and saw Avery. She gave me a faint covert smile, then switched her eyes away. I wondered if she had seen them, Tim and Pritchard. Probably. Vaguely, all along, I had intended to ask Avery to stay in town with me for a day or two; had more or less taken it for granted that she would, and now it all fitted into place. But then I glanced at Portia, still watching me, still eager. Good Lord! I couldn't ask her. Anyway, Mother had made a face behind her back the one time I had risked bringing her home. Only even Mother was above doing anything to hurt her. But this time Mother wouldn't be there, and Portia knew. She'd read the telegram. She was unquestionably expecting to be asked; her whole face said so. She was counting on having a ball, especially since now she knew I had some real live men, for a change.

"Stop chewing on your cheek," she whispered, and tried to pull my hand away from my face. I could have slapped her.

That was when I decided definitely I wouldn't ask her; she had just relieved me of the necessity. I gave her a really killing look, but she just bared those rather yellow teeth at me in return. What a creature! And to think I'd shared the same room with her for a whole year! Ever since they had decided that Joyce and I were "too close" and should each have other roommates, as a matter of fact. I looked at the malevolent little beast, and wondered if she could tell from my face how much I loathed her. Instead, she gave me the happiest of smiles; she was a regular sunbeam.

Because all of this was going on, Portia had to nudge me when it was finally over. "Get up, you silly ass!" she said, smirking and simpering in such self-satisfaction that I could have wrung her neck. We marched out, just as we had marched out of chapel every day that year, to the same old music. "You would think," Portia commented, "they would at least play something cheerful. Just this old grumble piece."

"Oh, die young! " I told her impatiently and brushed past. Even though she lumbered after me, I knew she was smarting with hurt feelings, and I was sorry in a way, but I didn't care in another. She was determined at any cost to get that introduction.

I still don't know how Avery found Timmy and Pritch so fast, but there she was when we came out, standing in the hall talking to them. She was laughing a great deal, it seemed to me. Then, before I knew it, Timmy had grabbed me and was kissing me, full on the mouth; kissing me the way people kiss when no one is around. I liked it, but I didn't. "My little Mole, my little Mole," he said over and over, and that gave me sort of a queer feeling. No one had ever called me "Mole" but Bart. But then I saw that everybody who passed by was staring at us, admiringly. I knew what they said about Avery, all the same, and just for a fleeting instant I felt a slight recoil; but what did it matter!

Gaily Avery threw an arm around me. "Oh, Lord Jesus!" she cried, "I'm OUT. Free! Free! Forever!" She then stuck out her tongue in the direction of Miss Fleming's back. I understood her elation, but I certainly could not join in; I had too much to cope with.

"Look," I said, "I have to dash. Mother is going away and the only chance I'll get to talk to her is on the way to the airport."

"Oh, that bit," Timmy remarked. "We've already fixed that. Pritch and I went by there before we came here. As a matter of fact, I thought you would be at home. We saw Corny. Had a long talk with her, as a matter of fact. In point of fact, she said there was no need for you to come straight home just to see her off—"

"What's all this 'fact' bit?" Avery put in.

"—She said she'd left you a portfolio of instructions with Tennie. Tennie's my girl, baby doll!" he cried. "Why didn't you tell me about Tennie?" I must have looked bewildered, and Tim's restraining hand on my arm momentarily annoyed me. I felt I was on a runaway horse, couldn't get off and was traveling at a high rate of speed. First it was "Mole," then calling my mother "Corny"—a privilege she allowed *no* one—arranging all my plans for me, then appropriating Tennie, and mildly rebuking me for not having revealed her sooner. There were oceans of things I hadn't revealed. How could I have, in that space of time? How well did we know each other after all? A scant forty-eight hours together and three special delivery letters. Also, whatever had made him go to my house in the first place? He had known I was at school; he had addressed my letters here. I distinctly did not like it. I should have said so. I didn't.

"Just the same," I told him, moving my arm away, "I want to go home. I've got some things to tell Mother even if she hasn't any to tell me."

Tim whooped with laughter. "Spirit! Talk about spirit, man! This woman's got it!" It was a little embarrassing, it was so unfunny. Pritchard looked like a graven image, and Avery wore only the faintest of appreciative smiles. She looked at me, very tellingly, as if to say, "See what I mean?" Then I remembered Portia.

She had sort of backed away, and was standing off in the

corner as if at any moment she would suck her thumb. She had big lamps for all of us, taking it all in. "Hey!" I said, and she came forward and was introduced. She couldn't have gotten anything out of it, for Pritchard was perfunctory, looked right through her, and Tim was downright rude—because she was identified as my roommate, I guess, and it must have frightened him. Still, she left us rather reluctantly, and Tim couldn't wait to ask me where I'd found the troglodyte. "Can't everyone have a troglodyte for a roommate," he said merrily.

"No, I suppose not," I answered. "I'm just one of the lucky ones."

III

Refusing to be coerced, wheedled, or tempted, I left Tim and Avery and Pritchard and went home to see Mother off. This was brief but excruciatingly painful, a sort of minor but terrible operation, and after I came back from the airport I convalesced in the bathtub for almost an hour even though I would be late meeting them at the Oak Room of the Plaza—the Palm Court was out: no one, they decided, really wanted tea. *I* did. Why hadn't I spoken up? I not only wanted tea, but I wanted, or had wanted, tea with Tim. Those crazy little tea sandwiches and tea, then maybe even a pastry—with Tim. Instead we would be having drinks—all of us. We would be a laughing foursome, and the intimate sort of "togetherness" I had envisioned seemed like a romantic idea lifted from, say, Portia's repertoire.

Joycie wouldn't have thought it cruddy. Joycie! But Joycie wouldn't have thought. Joycie was busy, off thinking about herself....Was everybody? Was I the only person who thought about anybody, ever missed anybody, ever needed anybody? All my life, I decided, had been an acceptance. First Mother, then Bart, then Joycie, and now I was accepting something else; accepting it completely, and maybe, as

93

Mother had said in her deft scalpel way, accepting the completely unacceptable. "Who was that nasty little creature who bowed and scraped and insinuated himself into my house?" she had asked. "He stood there grinning as if I were his next of kin! And such elegant manners! Such solicitous deference! Is he a hired assassin, or a mad doctor? I asked myself. Then he said he was your friend and proceeded to roam around my house like an auctioneer." After that, how could I tell her I loved him?

I got up, from my bath. The only logical thing to do was to dress, meet them, then try to think, judge for myself. Who was my mother to judge? She had a bright opinion about everything, but her life was proof enough for me she was wrong, wrong, wrong, And if she was so right, why did she always leave me? Even before I got past the bottom layer of clothes I decided that the whole thing had been off the top of her head, a last-minute caprice, a spurt of playful malice.

That afternoon I put on extremely simple white underthings. I thought of them, as I was dressing, as virginal, the raiment of sacrifice, but they were more than that. They were little-girl underclothes—things I had really outgrown, as I become painfully aware later when I discovered that my bra was too tight, and the straps of my slip ate into my shoulders. Over them I put on a dress I would not have dared let my mother know I owned. It was a cocktail dress, a real one, and my mother frowned on such inclusions in my wardrobe; said if I wanted to play "grownup" she would be glad to supply me. And to finish it off, I put on a terribly chic and fragile little hat, and as much lipstick as Avery wore.

But it wasn't until I had successfully got past Tennie and Kathleen and was in a taxi on my way that I felt really excited. I studied my face in a purse mirror with more than reassurance; I felt supercilious with pride and exotic; rare. And when I entered the Plaza I felt so grand and so stunning that I almost feared for my life. If anyone then had touched me I would have splintered apart into a million pieces of priceless crystal.

"God, get *her!*" Avery greeted me. She was sitting between the two boys, dressed rather casually for Avery, not even wearing a hat, just her long hair combed out over her shoulders into a feathery cream-colored fan.

I smiled austerely and Tim took my hand in a sort of Hollywood-marked gesture of tenderness. He gave me a slight kiss on the forehead which I felt was phony, but loved all the same. It seemed to fit the rest. The afternoon, my friends, seemed made out of some dazzling, tinsely stuff, and it did not distress me that it was cheap, unreal; I found it wildly, madly exhilarating that the day and the people had the mad good sense to wear it.

"Get you, you're stinking Maude!" I replied to Avery, and Tim screamed with delight. Then he and Avery began to talk about Bea Lillie's new record, and how it was all the rage. I remembered vaguely that the expression which I had just used with such captivating success was my mother's dozens of times over and, had probably first been Bea Lillie's. But Avery *was* stinking. Her pale eyes didn't focus quite right; or rather, they focused too intently and for too long, they were the glass eyes of a doll, and seemed milky.

Tim and Avery were making a lot of noise. They chattered and shrieked. I had a sudden air-pocket of depression, but no one around us seemed to mind. Looks—if any were actually directed at us, that is—were kindly. And once Pritchard accidentally touched my hand, and left his there for a moment, so I started feeling crazy all over again.

"Am I staying with you?" Avery flung her head around to say at some point.

"Certainly!" I affirmed recklessly, and recalled my mother's last-minute words on this subject, as if they had been from a textbook of a course I'd already passed. She had said, probing, "—I can't say I'm sorry you didn't drag that roommate home, but lovely as I have no doubt Avery Cowles—Stafford—whatever they call her—is—she couldn't be anything but splendid in contrast with the reputation her mother had—do not, and I mean it, Chloe, do not take up with her—seriously. School is out now and you can find other friends. Besides, her grandmother is crazy, and the first thing you know they'll have you out in that gigantic warren in Southampton. Old Mrs. Cowles is the original March Hare."

But Mother was in Capri, or would be by the time Avery and I went home. I told Tim yes, I did very much want another martini.

After one sip, however, I was glum. It was my third drink. And as we went on, I felt more and more as if I were on some sort of amateur air trip—alone in a balloon—surging upward, or plummeting. My spirits were alternately those of the classic party poop and the noblest of drinkers. Tim said he was glad to see I was a game girl with a good liquor I.Q., and I smiled blindly and did not tell him I had exceeded it. He also said he liked a quiet girl which, with my swirling wits, was all I trusted myself to be.

Not so Avery. Martinis made her very scintillating.

I dimly thought of things to say from time to time, and even said a few which Avery and Tim seemed to find howlingly funny, but for the most part energy and opportunity existed separately. Pritchard drank little and smiled even more infrequently, so perhaps he noticed, but then he isn't the sort who calls attention to others' defections. Anyway he was slightly angry at them. Avery had worked him over about an awful Southern girl named Vashti who was crazy about Elvis Presley and revival hymns, and Pritch. He denied knowing her, said he was serious about his religion.

This had brought down the house. "I suppose you'll deny that you told Lesley Bradford that Vashti Dunham thought 'I Come to the Garden Alone' was a rock 'n roll song. If you knew Vashti well enough to say that I'd say you knew her!"

"I said she was a spook, that's all," Pritchard said.

"And you didn't go to church with her last summer?"

"Once or twice."

Avery and Tim just broke up. "What makes you so ape?" Tim asked her, but he reached for my hand as he said it, and I didn't mind if he looked at her with real admiration. "Oh, I'm a throwback," she said, giving Pritch a malicious look. "I hate filter-tips and Elvis Presley. I'm old vintage. Cocktails, sophistication, late mornings, Arpege—"

"Chanel No. Five." Tim winked at me.

"—Don't be an ass—and I like things that tear you up and make you over. I'm no health girl."

"A resident of Miltown?" Pritchard said with sort of pathetic sarcasm.

"You sound strange and wonderful," Tim told her very admiringly, ignoring Pritchard. "Are you the same girl I used to know?"

She gave him a faint deprecating smile and a shrug. It had great charm. "I'm me," she said simply. When Pritchard got up to go to the john, she commented, to no one in particular, "Why is it so many boys like Pritch—boys our age, I mean— look unfinished—"

Tim gave a peculiar little laugh. "You can't mean me," he said. "I'm finished. I'm an old boy."

"And I'm an old girl," she said with seriousness.

I could have said something, could have called attention to the fact that they were getting maudlin, but they fascinated me, and I had lived too long with my mother to deny such drunken verities. Tim *was* an old boy, and Avery was an old girl. They had made themselves that way. And in that moment I suddenly adored them, abstractly, as if they were entwined hearts on a valentine addressed to me. The thought made me very sober and wise, much, much soberer and older and wiser than they.

"I'm hungry," I said, as Pritch was returning.

"All right," Tim replied pleasantly, but with no enthusiasm. "We'll feed you."

"I have to go," said Pritchard.

"Aw, sit down," Tim told him. "We're just ordering an-other round."

"Not me," Pritch shook his head. "I'm underage. You want me to drop you anywhere, Chloe?"

"I'll drop *you*, man, anytime!" Tim cried. "Sit down now, goddammit! Besides, you left your car up there by that cruddy school these two fleshpots go to—"

"*Went* to—" Avery corrected him.

"Oh, okay," said Pritchard.

I gave Pritchard a vague smile, feeling very faraway, and not exactly happy. I didn't know quite why. My mind, my memory, now behaved the way Avery's eyes looked. It stood still too long; and when prodded off, like a thing on a rock, it lost its bearings, then finally recovering, leaped to safety on a spot exactly like the one it had left. Pritchard wanted to go. It grieved me. Tim was now calling Avery "Ovary"; that caught at me, my sensibilities snagged on it like silk on a rough board. Their laughter sounded ugly. Pritchard looked stupid. Avery looked "coarse," as my mother said about women sometimes, and Tim looked weak. Pritchard had wanted to "drop" me—why? Why? I was with Tim. Tim didn't love me. Pritchard looked unfinished and scared. Avery looked old, old, old, as old as my mother. Tim looked as if he were holding a package from the drugstore, not my hand. Pritchard looked pouty, prudish, disapproving. Avery looked vulgar. Tim didn't love me, did not, did not—!

"What are you crying about, baby?" was the next thing I remembered. We were in a taxi, my head was in Tim's lap.

"Where is my hat? Have I lost it?"

"No, baby. Avery has it. She'll give it to you when we get there."

"Where is Avery?"

"They're right behind us. This is one of those tandem-type cabs. Seats two, and you needed to stretch out."

"They're in another taxi right behind us?"

"Yes, doll, right behind us."

"Where are we going?" I said. "I want to sit up."

"'21,'" Tim told me, helping me to sit up. "You said you wanted to go there."

I didn't answer. I wanted to go home. "I'm sick," I said.

"Again?" Tim asked. "Avery said you barfed your teeth out before."

I did? I thought. Well…An accomplished fact. There it was…I had done the unspeakable. I accepted it; took it as if he had told me I had died. There was no use asking him if he still thought I was any of the things he had thought before? I was so miserable that I resented his being there, beside me, taking care of me. He was sitting up with the dead.

Dinner passed. I was more conscious of Avery jamming my hat on my head than eating my food; I was more conscious of the fact that the headwaiter bowed and smiled when he recognized me than I was of what Avery said to Tim and what Tim said to Avery, or what anybody said to me.

I think I came to, really, in the Stork. Then I knew that Avery was really bombed. We were in the ladies' room and she was somehow putting on another dress. She tore the one she had on, and someone, probably was trying to help her, trying to calm her down, a little terrified at the vehemence of

Avery's anger. I wanted to ask her why she was so angry, what we were doing there, why she was changing clothes. She snatched another dress from a rack, when she finally had the first one off. "I'll show that billy sitch," she muttered over and over, and her hand trembled when she got around to putting on more make-up. I guess she told me, somewhere during the course of all this, that someone had come in wearing a dress just like hers; hence she had repaired, with me, to the ladies' room to change—into one of a dozen other things she always kept there. I was awed, almost shocked. Then we were back and she lurched against the table just as we sat down. Pritchard jumped up and grabbed her arm to steady her. Then I don't remember much. Just lots of taxis.

Tennie opened the door, for I didn't have a key. I remember her eyes, and I distinctly remember that she didn't say a thing, just left the door wide open and walked away. We went in the den, and when I woke up they were playing my Ella Fitz records. I was on the couch, and Mother's card table, all neatly cleared off, was right there, as she had left it. Gone. Gone. What had she said? You won't have such a bad summer in town now that we have the air-conditioners. What a lousy thing to say! I sat up, blinking.

"There's my little girl," said Tim, gleefully coming from the bar with what was apparently a fresh drink in his hand. "How's my little barf baby?"

"Fine, fine," I told him. He gave me a sip of his drink and put his arm around me.

"You're a goof-off, Longtree," Avery called. She and Pritch were sort of dancing, or rather dancing around each other, making sinuous movements, half taking the music seriously, half mocking it, not really listening.

"She's a sweet barfer," Tim said, "and I won't hear a word against her."

"Oh, die young!" Avery told him. "You and your sordid love affairs."

She twitched around an exaggerated Hawaiian-like movement. "You've got hips like a beagle hound," I heard myself saying to her in a rather flat, musing voice. It surprised me.

"You haven't got any!" She spun around. "You're built like a snake."

"And you weren't even built," I retorted. "You just accumulated."

Tim and Pritch loved it. Pritch bent over and held his sides. Avery gave me an uncertain smile. I still couldn't quite believe I had said it. And, as usual, it wasn't that funny. "Why do you laugh all the time?" I asked Tim quietly.

"To keep from crying," he said still laughing, and all of a sudden I knew it was the truth.

"I'm sleepy," I announced.

"Again?" asked Pritch.

"All you've done all night is barf and sleep," Tim said, but not unkindly, "and hell, it isn't even daylight yet. You can't be sleepy."

I looked at him. His face was open, but sort of oily, sort of nasty, like my mother had said. You're my first date, I thought, notwithstanding Pritchard who was now less real than an ad, standing there beside Avery. He hadn't counted. Tim did. Yet I was still sleepy. "I'm sleepy," I said.

"Where's your bassinet?" he asked, and added, "Baby," in a wrench of sarcasm that was as hard on him as it was on me.

"Drown it, Tim," Avery said. "Where is your room, sweetie?" she added to me. "I'm sleepy too, so tell me where I sleep."

"I'll show you," I said, much too gone to give directions, especially since she had never been here before.

Later I could never be sure that it was real or that I had imagined Tim had said to her, catching her hand as she helped me out the door, "Your room is my room." But I know he caught her hand.

IV

It was a gigantic warren, the Cowles' house out on Long Island, just as my mother had said.

How we got out there remains severely unreal and almost criminally joyous. We went in Pritch's car, one of those Nash things with the top that folds back like a hood on a raincoat. And we left that morning. We went to bed, and got right up. Tennie shook me, shook me angrily. "Tony's got that 'un's car," she said, her Baltimore accent getting thicker than ever as it does whenever she's upset.

I'm sure I looked dazed and un-understanding, which I was. "Go on, git up! Rip and tear! Run wild! See if I'll tell her on you!"

At last I must have managed to ask her what she was talking about, because then she showed me the note. I recognized Tim's handwriting. "Oh, keepers of the Longtree Zoo!" It started. "Tell whatever-his-name-is that Mr. Allyn requires his car at the first ray or frown of dawn—that is to say, 7:30. We mean it! One and all!" Signed, "Lochinvar, Prince of the Night, Prince of World travelers, Prince of House Guests and Special Favorite to Miss Chloe. P.S. Please have the car brought around by 7:30."

I handed back the note and started getting up. Tennie was seething. "I ain't gonna give you no breakfast," she said, as if she were denying something I'd asked for. "You can have your orange juice and coffee."

How many times I had heard her threaten my mother, when she disapproved of her, in precisely the same way! I, too, was breaking her heart. But this was a dim knowledge. And, like my mother, I ignored her just then; it came to me by rote, how to deal with Tennie. That morning, for the first time, I knew I was adult.

Tony had the car on time. And even when I saw Tim take three unopened fifths of bourbon from the bar, it struck me as the right and wise thing to do. Pritchard would drive. Tim and I crawled into the back, and he supplemented my comfort with a shawl, well tucked in, all around. Tony watched us shoot off his face full of amazement.

"Oh, you kid!" Avery called to me, her voice almost lost against the wind, as she grinningly tied a scarf around her head. I knew, rather desperately, rather magnificently, that I was still drunk. And I also knew that Avery had slept alone, that Tim had occupied Bart's room.

Somewhere on the way, and we got off it a great deal, we stopped for hamburgers. The first place said it was too early in the day. But then it got later. Then we stopped for Pritchard to throw up, and the rest of us had Pepsi-Colas and the bottles rattled on the floor of the car all the way to Southampton.

I remember everybody flinging arms into the air, and the expression that day, as the sky began to clear and the sun came out strong and earnest, was "Eeeeeeeee!" It was an expression of purity, like a high wind, like the last stages of madness or blues. It was perfect. We all said it, screamed it, standing up, drinking from the bottle, nuzzled together, shivering, then drinking from the bottle for warmth. Sometimes we slept. And we all did these things—all but Pritchard. He was sour—sober, not having any fun at all. His only thought must have been to get us there and to get some sleep.

"Here it is! Here, Pritch! Here!" I remember Avery saying when I was in the middle of a doze. I looked up and there was a huge wrought-iron gate, the kind that seemed to be indigenous to France, and had an egregious look here on Long Island, America. It was a Raoul Dufy gate. Pritch stopped the car. "I'll jump out and open it," Avery said, and leaped to the graveled drive. "It sticks," she said, jiggling it. "No one can work it. Not that anyone tries to."

"You mean you don't have a gatekeeper?" Tim called, leaning out.

Avery laughed at him, pushing her foamy hair out of her eyes and fiddling again with the gate lock. "We don't even have a gatehouse. The city took that over for taxes."

I studied Tim's face in profile. It looked a little drawn. Then Avery got the gate open, and she made a bow of welcome and we drove through to the grounds. We waited for her just inside and she ran around and got back in the car. "Drive straight ahead," she said, "and don't turn off to the right up there because that leads to the drained lake."

"The drained lake?" Pritchard asked.

"Yes. Madre—that's my grandmother—had it drained.

Someone told her it had snapping turtles."

"And did it?"

"Yes. It had three."

"How deep was it?" Tim asked. "Isn't that a boathouse I see over there?"

"It was deep enough for boats. But don't look at it. Anyway you can't really see it from here. Wait until later," and she added, "maybe she'll even fill it up again eventually. Look at the trees," she said. "Some of them are very rare firs and things."

Obediently, transformed into tourists on a sightseeing tour, we gazed at the trees. The drive and the firs seemed endless.

"There's where the gardens were," said Avery. "Only the man we have now is part-time and can't begin to keep them up, even if he knew how to."

We looked in the direction she indicated and saw an expanse of lawn, bald in spots, with paths still visible, and grass growing high where it grew at all. "They were formal gardens," she explained. "Medieval. Grandpa studied all that."

"The Glory that was Greece, the Grandeur that was Rome," Tim murmured.

"Yes," she agreed. "But it was all fake anyway. It's just as well."

The grounds continued. It was uphill, and firs and pines grew and grew. Still no house. Then there it was; easily the biggest house I had ever seen. Mentally I began to compare it to a city block and ended up not knowing which was bigger. We had swept into the side driveway, the front one being instantly impassable because it was piled with dead leaves, even now in June. We got out at what proved to be the kitchen door.

We unwound. Tim helped Pritchard unload the car while Avery and I got out and stood around uselessly. Every now and then Tim would give a hopeful look toward the back door, then at Avery, but no one said anything, and it was clear no one would. Obviously, Avery did not have anyone to call to come get our things—or her things, really, for the day before she had loaded everything she had at school into the trunk of Pritch's car.

I felt sorry for them as they struggled. They both looked tired and irritable, and Tim's hangover was so apparent that it was like a secondhand face. I knew he felt like killing everybody. I sighed and exchanged looks with Avery, thinking how nice it was not to be a boy.

"Is that all?" Tim panted, seeing Pritch pause.

Pritch grunted, and Tim stood for a moment looking dazed, as if he couldn't remember where he was. A great dark lock of hair was hanging in his eyes; he looked absurd and girlish, as if he wore curly bangs. It broke me up, sort of. His fatigue and disappointment had replaced eagerness. Somehow everything seemed to indicate that this was the story of his life, entitled: "Tricked Again."

"Why don't we just take the things in the back?" Avery suggested. The use of the plural almost made me wince with anger, and I strode over and picked up my own bag and one of hers. "Yes, let's do take the things in the back," I said sharply.

Tim disengaged my hands from the luggage. "You aren't carrying anything," he told me.

Lightly, Avery ran up the steps through the surcharged atmosphere, and held the door open while the boys brought the things in.

We came into a huge shiny kitchen, immaculately clean. No one was there, but it was quite clear that someone gave it regular and loving care. I could not think that Avery and her grandmother lived there all alone. There must be someone to help them keep up this monstrous place—true, we had only seen the back and one side, so far, but my impression was of a huge square block of bricks and mortar, an institution, possibly for the genteel insane.

At that moment, I certainly shared Tim's feeling: I wished I had never come. Mother had known what she was talking about. It was ghostly in spite of the bright morning sunlight; it was a set from a play about Russian decadence, or better still, location for a movie of "The Fall of the House of Usher." We had just arrived in the morning instead of at night, that's all.

I longed for Tim and Pritch to finish their carting, to have them near me. Avery's grin at me from the doorway when she lit a cigarette and offered me one seemed unreal. I felt as if she had offered me poisoned candy. She stood watching the progress of the boys as they made trip after trip with her suitcases, cardboard boxes of books, pictures, tennis rackets, lamps, and even a pair of lutes.

I think it was after their last trip when they stood panting and dirty, just before going back to the car to see if there was anything else, that the three of us—just three, not Avery—nearly jumped out of our skins.

A very ebony ovoid head stuck itself around a distant doorway, as if extended on the end of a broom. Then it grinned and the whole figure, that of a young Negress, appeared. "Sheep done drowned in the swimming pool," it announced cheerfully.

"When?" asked Avery, as if she found this the most natural greeting in the world.

"Last night, Mr. Silvers say, but my Momma say that sheep been in there two, three days. It all swelled up."

"Oh, Mr. Silvers wouldn't know anything about it," Avery said.

The girl giggled. "He down there with all of 'em telling 'em all about it."

Avery nodded. "Does Madre know it?"

"Nome, she done gone to Hampton Bays to the Charity Bazaar."

"That's right," Avery reflected. "I forgot this was the day."

"Yessum," the girl answered agreeably, grinning at each of us with friendly inquiry as she waited.

"Is there any coffee, Benda, or anything, do you know?"

"Nome, there ain't," Benda said pleasantly. "Groceryman come and said that—"

"Never mind," Avery stopped her. "What about the sheep? Did Mr. Silvers take it out?"

"Nome. He say his bursitis bothering him too bad and to wait 'til Miz Cowles gets home."

"Where's Jake? Can't he do it?"

"He drove Miz Cowles into Hampton Bays. In the jeep."

"The jeep?"

"Yessum. Was all there was. Miz Cowles parked hers in town yestiddy and forgot it 'cause some ladies brung her home who was having tea here."

"Oh, Lord!" Avery said in exasperation, as if the whole rather incredible thing were an old story to her. "Tell Mr. Silvers to get that sheep out of there. Jake's probably not going to be back for hours, then it will be too late or something."

"He won't do it," Benda announced affably.

"Tell him I want to see him."

"I'll tell him," said Benda, "but he won't come. He'll just wander off in them weeds of his he calls his garden."

Avery looked at us, as if for help. "That sheep will probably be in there all summer," she said. "And I wanted to have some people over to swim tomorrow."

"We can probably fish it out," Pritch offered.

"You and Tim are too tired," Avery said, still frowning. But Pritch looked suddenly refreshed and relaxed, and above all amused. This was going to be an outing after all—much more than he had expected.

However, Tim still had a drawn look, as well as one of disgust. "Are all your people crazy?" he asked Avery. "What happened to Rachel, or whatever her name was? I remember her from that houseparty two summers ago. She seemed like a firm character."

"Oh, she is. Rachel's wonderful. She's Jake's wife," Avery explained, "and Benda and her mother just come in a couple of days a week. They're the crazy ones, and Mr. Silvers, the gardener—wait until you see *that* one. But Jake and Rachel are fine, only Jake is sort of cheaty. And then there's Horty, that's their daughter. We grew up together, and now she's a secretary in New York. Sometimes she writes letters for Madre too."

That must be a treat, I thought, judging from what I'd heard about Madre.

"Golly, maybe Horty will be out this weekend," Avery said. "I hope so."

"Horty. Was she the short dark one you said lived here?" Tim asked.

Avery nodded. "She's great, Horty is," she said to me. "I'd do anything for Horty and Horty would do anything for me. I nearly died when I first went to Chalmers and wanted to cash in my trust fund so she could come with me. Madre didn't seem to mind, but Rachel did. Wouldn't have it."

"What about all this junk?" said Tim.

"Leave it," Avery said in dismissal. "Oh, no, wait! Let's get that bourbon first. If we can't have coffee, at least we can have that. Anyway, we should hide it. Madre pretends she's a teetotaler. Keeps all the liquor locked up except for cocktails before meals, and then has to be begged to have one herself."

"Don't you have a key?" Pritchard asked her, entranced. It was clear he was beside himself with wonder and amusement, as if he had just stumbled into a drawing room play that was very witty. He didn't seem tired at all.

"Of course I have a key, but she doesn't know it," Avery returned. "Often I meet her in the dead of night when we're both stealing down for the same purpose."

Pritchard laughed his head off, but I thought, ludicrous as the whole thing was, that it must be very sad for Avery. First, it was quite apparent that they had no credit with the groceryman, had louts for servants, lived in a gigantic old ruin of a house; then to top it off, she was not only an orphan, but had a March Hare for a keeper. Poor thing. No wonder she was fond of bourbon, martinis and Horty.

"I want to go see this drowned sheep," said Pritch.

"Aren't you tired?" Avery asked.

"Not any more. I'm having too much fun," he said.

"How about some bourbon?"

"Not for me," said Tim. "I want to sit down somewhere. Or fall down."

"Let's go see the sheep," Pritch suggested.

"You go. I'll abide."

"Chloe?"

"I want to see the ladies' room," I said. "Awfully."

"Here, right off here." Avery showed me.

When I came out I glanced into the kitchen as I went by, but it was empty again, so I wandered on, vaguely wondering where they were making the bourbon, or if they had taken their drinks with them out to the watery graveside, and where that was to be found. I crossed an enormous dining room, entered a reception hall with double curving stairway and chose a likely door off to the right. Beyond, I could see a screened-in side porch with cretonne-covered wicker furniture. All very comfortable. I found myself in a small room lined with bookcases, and off that was another spacious room; it appeared to be the drawing room. I walked its length and looked out of one of the tall wide windows. Beyond was a terraced lawn, and a great crater at the foot of it. It must have been an acre in width—the drained snapping-turtleless dry lake. Now it was lined with great cracks, and mud cakes curling up like Biblical tablets, waiting to be written on, or blank books from the unearthed Assyrian libraries. The log boathouse, on the farther shore, was still surrounded by stranded boats.

"What is all this?" Tim asked, joining me. "I've been looking at it from the front. Hasn't the old lady got any jack?"

"I don't think she could have," I murmured.

"Come look at it from the porch. Very vistaful."

"Vistavisioned?"

"Very." He took my hand, and together we stepped out onto the huge expanse of veranda. It was colonnaded like an antebellum house. Bigger than life, bigger than Hollywood.

"Where is the sea? The good old Atlantic?" Tim asked. "Is this really Long Island or old Virginny? These people must have had horrible indigestion when they built this dream house."

"It's horrible," I said. "Poor Avery."

"But look at all the ground she has to lose herself in."

I looked, but it didn't seem quite enough. And now Tim was sneering at her too, when only hours before he had been gone on her, all eyes.

"I thought you knew Avery pretty well before," I said.

"I came to some kind of houseparty out here once a couple of years ago," he told me, holding my hand again. "It didn't seem to have so many ruined gutters on the roof then, or servants like that whoever it was, escaped from the State Hospital."

"You like things, don't you?" I asked.

"I like you," he said intimately.

I wondered if he did. How had he showed it? He was a strange boy, but then, really, what did I know about him, or about anybody? New York and Mother and Bart seemed last century.

"I think the old lady has probably sold all of her paintings. Fabulous paintings," he said, "and silver too. The dining room looked stripped."

Now I knew what Mother had meant about the auctioneer. Tim *did* appraise everything. It made me unhappy, and I was just on the point of suggesting that we find the swimming pool, when he said, "Why is it you've never asked me any questions, baby doll?" He tightened his hold on my hand.

I looked at him. "Such as?"

"Where did you grow up? What are you?"

"All right," I said. "Where did you grow up, to take first things first."

"Everywhere."

"That's specific."

"Okay," he laughed, not looking quite so sure. "I grew up in Boston for one. In Panama for another. And then a little here and a little there…my family once had a place for the summer on Block Island—that was awfully hard to get to— and at Watch Hill, another time, Newport, still another, Palm

Beach in the winters—"

"But where did you grow up?"

"I haven't, my baby girl dolly." He grabbed me and squeezed me.

For a second or two I did not want to talk, then I knew I couldn't, even if I wanted to, but I still wanted to know. He went ahead, a released record I'd never heard, but had said, in curiosity, I wanted to hear.

"I was a blue baby," he said. "So blue that I was pronounced D.O.A.—Dead on Arrival. But my mother was sentimental, wanted to keep me around, having had no others who even got that far, and so I was swathed in swaddling clothes and put in the parlor, or whatever it was, and left to attract the attention of the wet nurse who screamed when she found me alive. After that, I was a pretty special thing. I talked at eight months, walked when I found some place to go to, and was a genius at seven. I read all of *Plutarch's Lives*. Then I began to paint pictures, and at about the same time learned to sleepwalk. We had a house at Oyster Bay then, and they used to leave fresh canvases and paints out for me so I could paint in my sleep if I felt like it."

"Did you ever feel like it?" I asked, so entranced that I felt like a sleepwalker myself.

"Yes," he said. "I did. I'll show you some of the canvases when we're married."

"Married!" The word whirred through my head; went so fast that it had no meaning.

"Tim," I said, "I'm—well, I'm not even seventeen—"

"I'm not even twenty-five," he said, "but I know what I

want. Shall I wait for you? Say, until you're twenty?"

It was broad daylight there on that colonnaded veranda. I told myself this as I looked at his serious eyes—they were gray—and his face, which was pale, but not gray: it looked healthy; it looked as serious as his eyes. Suddenly he was kissing me, to seal the pact, or to make the pact, as I had said nothing, and my mother, my sixteen years, and my life, were swept away in a tide of over-powering yearning. "Will you go to bed with me when we get upstairs?" he asked. "Will you?"

I nodded, but even as I did so I thought of many, many things, and knew I had to be alone before I could go to bed— to sleep—with anybody, even myself.

V

Anyway, there was, immediately, no time to go to bed. No time to sleep, no time to think. Tim and I had our last chance for dreams as we strolled in off the porch, not speaking, but holding each others' hands in the fierce possessiveness of that first knowledge of what it was to be together, what it was to think of someone else in the future, as one thought of oneself. I felt as if I were still whirling around inside—a clock that had been made to operate in the opposite direction.

"There you are," Avery said to us. "Where have you been? Communing with your own natures?" She was standing in the reception hall, and Pritch, grinning at us, stood in the doorway of a room which proved to be the sitting room, the one where the bar was.

We heard a car come zooming up the drive. It skidded to a stop, and as the ignition was being turned off, the motor roared as if the driver wanted to be sure the motor was still there, in perfect working order. "That's my Grandma," Avery said. "She drives that thing like an airplane."

The screen door slammed, and a deep musical voice called, "Avery! Avery! Avery! Avery!" and continued, as if it were deranged or chanting.

"Here, Madre!" Avery ran to meet her.

They met each other in the hall, just off the porch, and they bundled together in greeting, arms entwined, so that I could not see Mrs. Cowles. Then she was released.

Madre came forward, blinking behind bifocals, her lemon-gray hair like a tattered cap of lace around her head, her mouth turned up in one of those awesome false smiles that dowagers are supposed to wear, and sometimes do. She was short, as short as her granddaughter, and was dressed in an indescribably ill-fitting sweater and skirt. On her feet were a pair of shoes that were ancient enough to have been museum pieces, muddy enough to have come in from the farm, and as manly as a muscle. She was a perfect sight.

Graciously she acknowledged the introductions, apologized for looking "so informal," and went into a long derring-do tale about how she had dashed all over the country in her mud-bespattered Studebaker—"a sturdy little car"—which she had ran across "quite by accident in town. I'm such a damn fool. I forgot the thing yesterday"—in pursuit of that "scoundrel Billy Rivers."

"He's fed the horses oats again, love," she confided to Avery as we drifted, open-mouthed, toward the sitting room. "I know he has. I saw their stools, and I told him, distinctly told him, I did not want those horses to have oats. Did you see the babies?" she asked changing the subject.

We were now on the point of sitting down.

"No," said Avery. "Pritch and I have been out to the swimming pool to look at the dead sheep. Are there many?

What color? Maybe Chloe would like a whippet baby. But I forgot: your mother likes cats, doesn't she?"

"Cats," sniffed Mrs. Cowles. "I never knew Cornelia liked cats. She could have had the whole lot of your mother's Angoras, Avery, only I suppose they would have passed on by this time. What sheep—swimming pool—what are you talking about? I don't keep sheep. Drat that Mr. Silvers! Was it his sheep? I'll fire that maniac." She turned to us. "Oppie Smithfield told me last year about this wonderful gardener she knew of—a landscape gardener, and just what I needed—and now this person has attached himself here. Just comes and goes. Plants things nobody's ever heard of and ignores what else is growing, and then sits himself down in my drawing room for hours and expects me to listen to him. Drinks beer. Out of cans. Strutted right in with one in his hand, and I can't imagine that Rachel gave it to him. Just helped himself out of the ice chest. Talk! On and on, about Lady-this and Lord-that that you can be sure never heard of him, and his experiences in South American jungles. And I *know* Aggie Blanton never laid eyes on him. I asked her. She wouldn't let a thing like that near her garden, even if his hands were tied—She has fabulous gardens, my dear—"

I looked at Tim. He was sitting dumbfounded and discomfited, but Pritch was grinning, following every word, and Avery was smiling indulgently, benignly: this was home.

"—Let's go look at the whippets." Mrs. Cowles jumped up. "And maybe Rachel will get us a nice lunch together and we can have a picnic. You'd like that, wouldn't you, love? We can drive up to Scotdale. The grounds are lovely. Of course, we can't go in the house, so it will have to be a cold lunch. The chipmunks ate the floors away," she added to me in explanation. "I'd just had it redecorated too. All they left was a small section of the living room, so the grand piano is still intact. Ate all around it. Not very musical I would say, ha! ha! but they certainly devoured everything else. You'd think hardwood floors would discourage them. They're avid little beasts, though. All the upper floors fell down, or rather all the furniture did. On top of some of them. Served them right. Nasty little bodies and skeletons everywhere when we discovered it. Of course I should have made the trip up there before, it's to be Lovie's house, you know, but I just returned myself, and who would think that Jake would simply let things go the way he has. That man is going to end up owing everything I have. I told him so today, love. And he just saw fire, but he knew it was the truth. I had to duck down by Matthews' Store when we went past. All because Jake ordered all those new bathtubs without even asking me, and of course I'm not going to pay the bill—*they* don't need new bathtubs...."

I stopped trying to follow it, and then I stopped listening altogether....I merely watched: the way Mrs. Cowles' jaw worked when she talked. It worked very vigorously. And I stole a glance at the others, all spellbound, even Tim. Mrs. Cowles had sat down again to finish—finish?—whatever it was she was saying. I forced myself back, trained my mind on her words.

"—It is *good* to have you home, and we will do no end of things this summer, although I'm rather tired. It was very tiring this winter. I bought a mountain of groceries, love, if you and your friends want to go get them. In the back of the car. Taormina was dull, dull, dull. Nothing but bridge all the time. And the weather was a disgrace this year. How are you? You look well. I see you've met some nice young people. Give my love to your mother," she nodded to me. "She was always so high strung. I see her name's still not back in the *Social Register*. I would have called her. I think it's an outrage the way they take people's names out when they change husbands too often to suit them. The Watch and Ward Society. But then I hear you're from Boston, young man," she said to Tim, "so I suppose you don't find any of this particularly shocking—"

"Indeed I do," Tim put in.

"Do you? Well, most young people simply don't care. They believe in mortality, not morality the way people used to. I find that shocking. But I really must show Lovie the whippets, and she must show me her sheep. You'll excuse us, won't you?"

"Come go too," Avery turned to us.

Pritchard hopped up dutifully. However, I did not, nor did Tim; it was fairly plain to me that distrait as old Mrs. Cowles seemed to be she wanted a word with her granddaughter. Such people, I knew, were usually extremely well-organized and astute on the rock bottom where it counted, and just crazy on top where it didn't matter. After all, my own mother wasn't exactly *Parents' Magazine*'s idea of the sane, functioning mother, but I defy them or anybody else to locate a parent who gets a higher percentage of "obedience"—i.e., her own way—from her offspring.

This line of thought pointed a direct arrow to Tim, sitting docilely beside me, once again covertly enfolding my hand as Avery and her grandmother, trailed by Pritch, left for the outdoors. I felt Tim's intent look, but just then I couldn't quite return it, so I studied his hand in mine. It was brown in contrast to mine, big, in contrast to mine, firm and strong, the skin texture more defined, weathered, protective, kind…but what was it doing there? What would my mother say when, and if, she ever decided to come back from Capri and found his hand, so to speak, in mine? In answer I had a sudden vision of a spray of sparks, a flash fountain of fire, crackling, spewing. Then dying out, cold and useless as last Fourth of July's sparklers. I remembered what she had once said in answer to something Bart and I, in concerted folly, had proposed doing: "Who would have ever thought that a peacock could be a mother to blind sparrows?" she had asked.

"What are you thinking, little Mole?" Tim asked softly, intimately, caressing one of my fingers.

"Of scorn."

"Scorn? That's the most unsuitable topic I ever heard of. Are you jealous just because I was admiring Avery's grandmama? I can't admire you all the time, now can I? It would be very limiting."

This surprised me very much, and I turned to gaze on him in my astonishment, and was immediately hugged. "Don't ever be jealous, little Mole," he cradled me, consoling me as if my look had given him proof that he was right. "I'll defect plenty of times, but I'll always come back to you."

This speech struck me as wayward, and I must have stiffened as he held me, for he stopped his tenderness almost at once. "Aren't you sleepy?" he asked, putting me aside.

I nodded, though I wasn't tired any more, really; hadn't been since we were on the porch.

"Let's sneak off together," he said. "Let's just go and lie down together some place. There must be a secret little room somewhere upstairs—"

I found myself shaking my head, very firmly, although the idea was so exciting and compelling that I had fully intended to nod in approval. I still don't know why my automatic reflex was so completely in the negative, but there it was.

"Come on," he coaxed. "They'll be back in a minute or two, and then there won't be a chance. Now we can get away with it."

I didn't even bother to argue, although my thoughts were rioting inside my head in a bid to be heard pro and con. I just silently continued shaking my head.

He was nonplussed. "You mean you won't?" His voice was bewildered and not happy.

I just sat dumbly, not looking at him, fingering his hand and gazing straight ahead at the cloisonné cluttering up the mantel.

"What's the matter? Are you scared?" He asked harshly, but the petulance also in his voice diminished the strength his anger might have had. "Do you like being a virgin? Frigid women—!" he made a noise of disgust. "I'm not going to beg you. I don't want anybody who doesn't want to—"

"I want to," I said quickly, again surprised at my own words, but I meant this as fully as I had meant my previous refusal.

He gave me a long, searching look, one combining doubt, hunger, sweetness and selfishness, and increased the pressure of his hand on mine. I felt as if I were slipping into a pool of ecstatic warm liquid.

I suppose anything could have happened if the others hadn't come back just then. It was perfect timing, as if someone had called "Break!" and we had sprung apart guiltily. But I also felt the relief mingled with anxiety I would have had had they also called "Cut!" And it struck me as all very unreal and a little ridiculous.

Tim had on his company face again and was sitting alienated from me, his own private person again, smiling and ready for group participation. Even his profile now left me cold; indeed the mere thought of him filled me with distaste, and I studied him as if he were an annoying absurdity.

Mrs. Cowles, a cigarette hanging out of the side of her mouth, which I came to find was part of her habitual appearance, sharply scrutinized us in a fleeting second, then flicked her eyes away. "Rachel hasn't been in?" she asked quickly in the face of Tim's banal smile. "I must go see about our luncheon basket if you children really want to go. Of course if you'd rather nap or take a run down to the beach—I had thought it might be nice to drive over to East Hampton this afternoon to Grove Beach, but there's plenty of time for that if you are tired—"

"No, no!" Pritch and Avery protested, and Tim joined in

just after. And all three at once insisted that we go on the picnic to Scotdale—why, I still can't imagine, and I'm sure they didn't know either. But it was certain that Pritch, in particular, was making an all-out effort to charm Mrs. Cowles, and Tim was right after.

Avery looked at me. "Chloe looks clobbered," she said.

"That's no way to talk, Avery!" Mrs. Cowles scolded. "The *expressions* I hear nowadays! What does it mean anyway? Clobbered."

"You can tell just from the sound what it means," Avery grinned, lighting a cigarette for herself.

"I certainly cannot! Does it have to do with dairy farming? When I was at Chalmers such language would not have been countenanced. We toed the mark, I can tell you. I'll never forget the time Miss Hoskins corrected me in chapel in front of everyone for whispering. 'It is nothing to me if you're a princess or a hodcarrier's daughter,' she said, 'In this chapel I am supreme.'"

"Oh, Madre!" Avery laughed at her. "You were probably dreadful."

"Of course I was," Mrs. Cowles agreed stoutly, a self-satisfied happy smile breaking over her face. "But nothing like your mother. She was the first girl in Chalmers who ever dared—and regularly, so she told me—to go west of Fifth Avenue whenever the fancy moved her, or to sleep through breakfast and those detestable morning constitutionals—trots, we used to call them. We were treated just like animals, fine racing horses. Up we'd go, two blocks, turn to the right one block, to the left on the next—"

"Why didn't you make a square instead of zigzagging?"

"Oh, we did my first year there, then an 'incident' happened on the second block down and it was promptly outlawed—"

"What kind of incident?"

"I can't tell you. It isn't proper."

"Now, Granny," Avery wheedled.

Mrs. Cowles frowned at her for the "Granny." "A gentleman relieved himself in one of the potted shrubs outside the Harper mansion," she said.

We were still giggling when she stood up, pleased with the success of her schoolgirl reminiscence. "Now you children entertain yourselves and I'll see about our picnic."

"They still make you take that morning walk, don't they?" Pritch asked Avery.

"They certainly do. We look like something out of that Bemelmans book—*Madeleine*, or whatever it is—cantering down the street in our uniforms, especially the big ones. You feel like an idiot."

"Do you?" Tim asked me.

"Wouldn't you?" I replied.

All of us were momentarily silent, musingly so, vaguely smiling at each other. I was thinking that Joyce had told me Bart always said that he had fallen in love with her, really, when she was in the Sixth and he had quite by accident seen me and Joyce smartly stepping along one morning in our daily drill, and that we were both too absorbed in it to look up and wave. Actually, we were just stupefied with boredom and in a hurry to get it over as quickly as possible. Bart often said that he had never known girls could walk so fast.

"Hulloo, hulloo!" This sound, startling us, echoed, as if from a loudspeaker with the volume turned up.

"Who's that?" Tim asked sharply.

"Oh, no!" Avery groaned, recognizing the sound.

"Who is it?" Pritch urged her.

"The Neck, I think," she said, "and Blossom Nefkin. And probably Mary Sellers White."

"What's all that?"

"Madre's," she groaned again. "Her crew. And if it is The Neck it means she's here for the summer."

Just then three ladies, two dressed in flowered silks, and one in chiffon drapes, including a cowl-like arrangement on her head that made her appear to be an escapee from purdah, came pressing in upon us, all wearing great happy smiles, as if they were grapecrushers, very pleased with the prospect of their work, and we the grapes.

VI

The picnic did not get under way until four-thirty: the cortege, that is, did not form outside the great iron gate until that time. The reasons for this delay were multitudinous and had precluded, among other things, our having lunch or even a snack, though Madre, as we now also called her, several times scolded us in a harassed voice for not fixing ourselves "a bite." This proved impossible. Tim and I personally made two trips to the kitchen; on the first, we were peremptorily dismissed by Madre for getting in Rachel's way, when we were peeking in the icebox. The second time we encountered Jake, who was scowling ferociously at his wife, Rachel, when we came in through the pantry. He turned his scowl on us, making it quite clear that we were interrupting a family argument, or a lecture. In any case, we gave up, and just drank.

The Neck (she of the draped chiffon) more or less set the pace for this activity. The thirsts of the Gobi Desert had apparently accompanied her and her other oriental trappings on this visit. She was altogether a curious woman. Avery had nicknamed her "The Neck" for a good reason: she looked like Alice after she had swallowed the "Eat Me" pill and had opened out like a "telescope"; this as a result of some kind of injury she had experienced in India when she was a young woman, and they had kept her neck too long in the cast. Anyway, she was veddy British, veddy Pukka-sahib, being the widow of an officer in the Indian Army, and talked endlessly about "Out There."

The Neck in fact, talked almost as much as Madre (who, fortunately, was out of the room most of the time), and tossed off her whisky neat (or with an occasional "just a splash") in short ladylike gulps between her hurried and incessant forays on "topics." "This is a topic which particularly interests me," she would announce frantically at embarkation point; or, "the Middle East topic is an extremely touchy one with you Americans—"; or, "my favorite Far East topic is…" Whatever the topic she discussed, the general heading of the afternoon's discourse could be labeled "Inja: Its English and Its Environs"; with "Yes, Just a Little One, Thank You," as a subtitle.

Tim and Pritchard found her fascinating, and if her companions did not, or had heard it all before they were at least subdued. Like painted flowerpieces, they silently adorned the end of a couch and an easy chair, respectively, and gave no sign of life, even plant life, except for occasional drooping nods of the head and slight shifts of the postures of their mouths, which seemed to have been created exclusively for smiling. Madre swooped in and out, frowning most of the time at The Neck, either for taking the floor too much, or taking the drink, and thus encouraging the corruption of the young, but her visits were, however overwhelming, brief.

I, for the most part, took a blurred view of all this. I distinctly was not used to so much bourbon, or so little sleep. But I felt very tranquil.

At four o'clock, Madre announced all was in readiness, and we stood up. The Neck, seeing us do so, merely raised her voice, making sure that this announcement should not cost her her audience, and we filed silently out into the hall.

"Oh, God's nightshirt!" Madre exclaimed at the front of the line. It seemed that the large picnic thermos holding the punch, which Avery had found an opportunity at some point to tell me she planned to spike, had leaked all over the Aubusson carpet, and when Madre angrily lifted the jug and shook it, it proved now to hold exactly nothing.

"Let's have wine!" The Neck cried gaily, waving her chiffoned arm in a holiday gesture that looked grotesque and unbecoming, so Jake, who was to drive the jeep, which would serve as the kitchen wagon in our train, was dispatched to the wine cellar.

"Like Omar!" The Neck exulted as we returned to the sitting room to wait. She then quoted several quatrains of the *Rubaiyat*, declaring that Oriental poetry was one of her "pet topics," whereupon Blossom Nefkin, who was always called just that, as if it were a double name, unprefaced by anything to distinguish her as a maiden lady or a woman with a husband, broke into a long erudite oral excursus on the merits of the Fitzgerald translation of Omar Khayyam, as opposed to four others which she, personally, considered superior and more faithful to the original.

"More in keeping with the feeling," The Neck said at last,

recovering from her astonishment at having been rendered speechless so long. "I do feel—yes, I uncategorically agree—that Fitzgerald loses a lot, a lot is lost in translation, so to speak."

"Do you know Sanskrit?" Tim asked innocently behind his smirk, for it was rather clear from The Neck's confusion that she hadn't dreamed there was more than one translation of the work in question.

The Neck gave him an austere but indecisive frown, cunningly inclined her head in such a way that the gesture could be taken either as an intention to rearrange the folds of her headcovering or as an answer to his question, and said to Blossom Nefkin that she should read Laurence Hope, since she "liked things Oriental"; especially the one about "Pale hands I loved."

Then Jake came in with two bottles of wine under his arm, and a stranglehold on the necks of two others. "My God! You're ruining it!" Madre exclaimed, and snatched the bottles away from him one by one, looking as if she would slap him in the face as soon as she had finished.

We drove down to the gate then, in a strange string. Madre in her "plucky little Studebaker" went first. The one called Mary Sellers White, incongruously seated in and piloting her Jaguar sports car, immediately followed. She drove the sleek beast as if she would not deign to take any notice of its crass high-powered mechanics, as if it were an electric with wall vases and fringed window-shades, or, better, as if she were being chauffeured and not driving at all. We came immediately after, while Blossom Nefkin and The Neck bore down upon us in a huge old Rolls, belonging to The Neck, that had evidently fallen sick and complaining from age and neglect, wheezed along behind us like a diseased and disgruntled dragon.

"Will it stand the journey?" Tim asked Avery, indicating The Neck's motorcar.

"Certainly; if it doesn't she'll whip it into submission."

Jake brought up the rear.

Setting the pace, Madre tore through the countryside and gamely the rest of us followed, a little astounded and certainly disbelieving, except for Avery, who found this a mere everyday, enjoyable lark. Had there been any hills and dales I could say we wandered, nay, rushed o'er them. Once or twice I thought Madre gave signs of stopping, but the slowing in pace was only a breathcatcher. Then, losing her bearings, as she explained later, having led us down a sandy deserted road, she brought the procession to a full stop just short of a potato field. All heads hung out of the cars.

"Sorry, sorry!" Madre called. "Lost my bearings."

"I should think so," The Neck returned irritably, and we all began backing out, for our lives, as Madre set her small car in reverse without warning.

"I thought she knew where she was going," Pritch remarked.

"Yes, I thought we were going to Scotdale," I said.

"So did I," Avery replied not in the least perturbed. "But I suppose Madre changed her mind."

Madre had changed her mind, and we never did get to where we were going because she forgot how to get there.

After several false maneuvers similar to the potato field exploration, we settled for a cornfield not far from Bridgehampton, one which belonged to God knows who and was bordered by a thicket of trees and poison ivy. But everyone seemed fairly contented and the picnic spot was pronounced a success.

Jake spread a large tablecloth over the corn stubbles and The Neck and Madre pointed out rocks for each of us to sit on. My rock was near Pritch, and not nearly so muddy at the base as was the one designated for poor Blossom Nefkin. Tim and Avery were put side by side.

"I do wish Mary Sellers had brought her mandolin!" Madre cried out happily, seated herself now, as the others were all disposed.

"Perhaps you'd like me to sing," The Neck offered and looked around the group smilingly seeking assent. There was a weak murmur of it.

The Neck immediately set up a dim but sorrowful mewling that apparently made the hair rise at the nape of Jake's neck, for he gave her such a look of startled reproach that I felt he was suffering a physical injury. He studiously applied himself to the cold beer which Madre had allowed him to bring along. The rest of us munched at our chicken and cucumber sandwiches and weakly watched The Neck in her apparent agony. Finally she was finished, and there was such general relief that she was heartily congratulated. When she threatened, through encouragement, to tune up again, Madre said in a loud voice, "Now, Mary Sellers, it's time for you to

do your handkerchief animals." And as if she had been standing in the wings all this time awaiting her cue, that lady
whisked a large white handkerchief from her purse and
quickly transformed it into bunnies, kitties, ferrets and something that Pritchard identified for me as a tree sloth.

By this time we had had lots of wine and the sandwiches
were almost gone.

I had a whole bottle of *liebfraumilch* to myself. This insured
the glow that had finally come at the end of the afternoon's
heavy drinking, a sort of rosy sunset feeling at the end of a
scorching hot day. I was certainly not drunk, but I was far
too blissful to be sober. This was especially true in the face
of the fact that Avery and Tim seemed inordinately absorbed
in whatever they were talking about, and somehow I didn't
really mind. Pritch and I were clearly forgotten—not even
discarded, just forgotten, and I regarded this situation with
the same interested tolerance I would have felt had I been
seeing it in the movies. When Pritch took my hand, I responded with absent warmth. The gesture seemed such a natural one for a couple sitting together in the movies.

I know now that Pritch took my hand through a sort of
defiance and desperation—I think to show the other two that
they couldn't do what they were doing to me; and to show
them they couldn't do what they were doing to him, for
though he had no jealousy about Avery, he had pride, and
they were violating the set-up by rudely pairing off together.
He symbolized her partner, and I symbolized Tim's, whatever the emotional involvement on a deeper level, and his
sense of propriety was injured. Madre and her guests were

not paying the slightest bit of attention to us now, and the four of us were again ourselves, no longer playing at being grown-up. Besides, The Neck was now quite drunk, Mary Sellers was on the verge of falling asleep, and I don't think Blossom Nefkin had ever been aware of us or of anything. The two of them trudged off together on a hike, and Jake had long since disappeared.

"I know where there's a wild strawberry bed," Avery said to Tim.

I felt helpless. "I know where there's a wild bed," Pritch murmured and watched as the two strolled off together, hand in hand. He looked after them in frustration. "Atkins can be very A when he wants to."

I didn't say anything, for honestly I still didn't much mind. Pritch rather awkwardly released my hand. "That one has faked out," he nodded toward The Neck.

Both she and Mary Sellers had. They were draped over each other, so relaxed that they looked as if they'd been thrown away.

"I don't go for these gone old girls," Pritch told me. "This whole session is lousy. Atkins is being very A. Are you firmed up on that noble actor?" he asked me. "Because if you are I think his behavior is pretty cruddy."

I studied him for a moment, puzzled at his concern. It was hard to believe he could have any. And it was harder to believe that this was the same Pritch who not too many months before had made me feel like a lead balloon. Bart used to whistle "Answer to a Teen-Age Prayer" every time Pritch's name had come up before. Now I knew why. He *was* sort of what they meant. He was everything a rock n' roll girl—that Vashti, for instance—would want: enigmatic, young, self-contained like a perfect robot, a work of economy. You knew what he was composed of, but you still didn't know what he was. I had lived around people like my mother too long to really go for him much, after the first flush. Now I plain disliked him. Now, too, having the situation pointed up through his having pointed it out, I felt angry and hurt at Avery and Tim. Even if I had not been "firmed up" on Tim, as Pritchard put it, his behavior, and Avery's, was still "pretty cruddy."

"I guess you don't want to talk about it," Pritch finally observed. I shook my head to indicate that I guessed not.

We sat silently, and I got off my rock and went over and selected a pickle from the picnic cloth. I bit at it thoughtfully and tried not to notice Pritch fidgeting. He was full of anxiety and couldn't sit still. He roamed up and down the picnic spot, his hands in his pockets, his shoulders slouched in a troubled way. I wondered what he had to worry about.

"This is a regular still," he announced to me. "What do they expect us to do?"

"Amuse ourselves," I told him quietly.

"The only thing that would amuse me is a trip back to civilization."

"I'm ready whenever you are," I said.

"Let's go."

As we went to his car I halfway thought we'd find Avery and Tim in it, but we didn't.

I was numb with apprehension and disbelief—at myself,

at them, at the whole crazy day.

Pritch let me help myself in the car, and I didn't care. "You want to go back to town?" he asked.

"I don't care," I told him, for none of it seemed to matter.

"Let's just drive and let the car decide."

I didn't bother to answer.

"You know, Chloe, Avery is not your sort of friend. She can't drink and she does. She doesn't believe in anything. When I first knew you, you didn't like her."

"Yes, I did," I said, and I wanted him to stop talking about her, about anybody. I had a few things I could have said.

"She's nineteen, you know. That's old. You're just sixteen. I remember. I even remember your birthday."

I wanted to be sarcastic, but I wanted most of all just to be quiet, alone. I had so many things to think of: Where are all the beautiful people? Where are all the beautiful people? kept running through my mind. When I was a baby I had always thought the beautiful people must be in Europe, on the Riviera, then I went there and they had gone. Then I thought they must be off skiing in Sun Valley and I went there and there were just lots of tired business-men in glasses with silver-blonde secretaries. The same thing with Florida and Nassau. Where were they? I wanted to ask somebody, but Pritch would be, I could tell now, the last one to know. Maybe Joycie knew. Maybe they were on the subways and in the suburbs, but I didn't think so. Joycie! Joycie and Bart! How I missed them—not together, but as I had known them, which was as separate beings. Then I fell asleep.

When I woke up we were at Montauk Point and I knew that Pritch was going to seduce me.

VII

It must have been around eight o'clock, because there was no sign of the sun. It had died while I had slept, and I awoke feeling very sad, as if a great part of me had died with it.

"You cold?" Pritch murmured. I could feel his arm around me and I wondered how long it had been there; how long we had been parked here. Idly, we sat in the open car and watched the fishermen on the beach as they stood in their hip boots, casting again and again into the darkening water, keeping faith with the fish. Some had their heavy fishing rods dug into the sand, or in one of those things they sell in sportsmen's stores, to hold the rod, the line treading the water far out, waiting. The fishermen looked as idle as we, but they were alert. And I was alerted too. I knew something was going to happen between me and Pritch; I was even fairly sure what it would be. I was even fairly sure what I wanted it to be.

"Do you remember what you said before we got here?" his voice was soft, and he caressed my shoulder.

"When?" I asked sharply. Hadn't I been asleep since we left the picnic? Is this what drinking did to the memory?

"Before you went to sleep the second time—when we— when we stopped and—stopped on the road."

"When did we stop on the road?"

He gave an easy laugh. "Don't tell me you don't remember. When you said you wanted to drive all the way out here."

"I shouldn't have," I said firmly. No wonder I had felt sad when I woke up to find the day was gone! What else was gone? What else?

"Look here, Pritch," I began. "I like you a lot, but I must have been sort of spiffed...."

"You shouldn't drink." He lighted a cigarette for both of us and handed me mine. The intimacy of the gesture terrified me. I wanted to get out and run and run—run my head off to safety.

"I want to go home," I said in a voice that was as large and as free from shivers as I could make it.

Silently he started the car and began driving out of the sand. I looked at him very puzzled. The line of the jaw on the rejected man is supposed to be "grim," "rigid"—all those things. He just looked placid, as nearly as I could tell. He also looked beautiful there in the moonlight. His hair now was not bright pale gold, but silver. I wished desperately for a drink, knowing at the same time that it might make it worse, and hated the taste of the cigarette I was smoking. I threw it away. Now what?

"It's just as well, really," he commented, once we were back on the road.

I dared not ask him what.

"But would you still like to drive over to East Hampton

to that party? We could have dinner first at that place that's the Pavilion in town...."

His arm was long since gone from my shoulder; both hands were his own again and on the steering wheel. It occurred to me all at once that I really liked him a lot.

"Did you really mean it," he asked, "when you said you thought it was right for me to go to Divinity school back in Cambridge? My family thinks I'm crazy, and my brother—he's very last century—says it's immoral."

"I don't know," I murmured, hoping to hide my complete confusion.

"I'm too gone on women, _he_ says—"

"Are you?"

"Chloe—I shouldn't be telling you all this, feeling as I do—"

How did he feel? I hadn't a clue. The thing I had felt for him—back in childhood, it now seemed—was so remote and unreal....

"—My brother says I'll turn out the same way as that Henry Ward Beecher character—too interested in women."

"Pritch, Pritch," I murmured, feeling lost with sympathy for him and squeezed his hand.

He returned this gesture with such power that I thought he would lose control of the car. He caught his breath and almost sobbed. "Chloe, Chloe, I want you, I want you! Is it wrong to want you? Tell me, Chloe, is it wrong to want you? Is it, is it?" he insisted.

"Pritch, Pritch," I replied, knowing nothing else to say. He had stopped the car abruptly at the side of the road and we clung together, kissing, his arms around me, trembling, imploring. Wave after wave of desire took both of us. I couldn't think, I couldn't reason. I could only feel. The most important thing on earth at that moment seemed to be to go off together into nowhere, all alone.

Frenziedly, he started the car, and we whipped back on the highway. We tore down the road, back toward the Hamptons. We held on to each other, his skin tingling against mine, his hands fiercely demanding in a way that I knew was what grown-up people meant by blind passion. Tim's attractiveness was nothing—a little wisp of fire, a burning leaf; this was overwhelming. I was mad for Pritch. I was mad for him in a way I felt I would never feel again, couldn't feel again. The urge for him was stronger than living, than thinking, than anything. All I wanted was Pritch.

After it was over was when I began to think about it, all it meant. But not then. When neither of us could stand it any longer, we drove off the side of the highway and Pritch took me. Not like a gentle rosebud, with no tenderness whatever, but in the way that I wanted him to take me: a wild beast making love to another wild beast. I didn't think about its being the first time—if it *was* the first time—or about its hurting, if it did hurt. I just wanted it, whatever it was like. And it was fierce and savage and all very quick like a jungle mating; neither of us said a word, at least not an intelligible one, and when it was over we just looked at each other for a moment, then Pritch started the car and we drove away.

My clothes were wrecked, but somehow I didn't care, and oddly I felt no guilt at all about what I had just done. Casually,

I went through the motions of combing my hair, adjusting my dress, straightening the seams of my stockings. But I might have been a cat licking its paws. This was the thing that dumbfounded me. I had taken to nature as easily as an animal. Objectively, my mother, for instance, would have said this was a very good and healthy thing, though she would not have liked knowing that her own daughter was capable of the good and healthy thing. Then why did I mind? And why had Pritch minded before it happened? I sat there in our silence curiously examining my thoughts, turning them over and over as if they were foreign bodies.

"How do you feel?" Pritch asked me at last; asked in the same way one would when inquiring about the health of one who has just had a tooth extracted.

"I don't know," I answered, giving an involuntary shrug which, of course, he couldn't see, but which I felt and which momentarily astounded me, in the same way I had been shocked to discover my own lack of guilt.

"I always knew you'd be like this," he said warmly, his voice full of appreciation, as if he considered me a good sport.

When I didn't answer, he continued, "Don't get me wrong. I didn't mean just how you *were*—you know, the way one of the crew would say when he makes out with a game girl—but the way you are now—good. Sound."

"Thanks," I murmured. He was trying to tell me he found me sensible, and was glad.

But was I? Was I either glad or sensible? I firmly knew that the last thing I would ever be was the easy type. Maybe

I wasn't in love with Pritch, but more in love with Tim and therefore owed Tim myself and had done this seemingly wanton, irresponsible..."Pritch!" I said suddenly. "Tell me something—something straight-arrow—"

"What?"

But I couldn't put it into words. Anyway, I knew the answer. "Nothing," I said. "Never mind." For even as I asked him it came to me why I would not just make love easy-come easy-go ever again: I had developed a sense of responsibility.

Or, perhaps, my sense of responsibility was something that had come built in, like ears and hands, and I had never had real need of noticing it before—and then only to violate it. Now I was filled with vast shame.

In the darkness, as we drove, I tried to persuade myself that this was not so, but just as the oncoming headlights seared the dark each time a car approached, so the truth lit up the thick bank of excuses I was able to build for myself. It was *not* true that I had taken Pritch out of jealousy over Tim's inattentiveness; nor was it true that I had leaped at the chance to take Pritch now because I hadn't gotten him the year before—the year before, at the tea dance, all he had wanted from me was to make out with me, and it had horrified me. No. I had done it because the urge had come on me, and Pritch might have been the gardener, the delivery boy, the man in the moon. There hadn't been a drop of romance in it! I had not lost my virginity because I wanted to lose my virginity *per se*. I had merely lost it, on impulse. It had been as self-destructive as stepping off a cliff to satisfy a whim to feel the sensation of falling; or picking up a live wire to see what it feels like to be electrocuted. In the future love-making for me would be definitive, and even if wild and crazy, at least I would be there, fully responsible.

This is what I told Avery hours later when we got back to Madre's.

Everyone had gone to bed and Rachel, her hair in curlers, looking disapproving and not too pleased at being waked up, let us in. We tiptoed up the wide staircase after her and she showed us our rooms. Mine adjoined Avery's, I found, after Rachel and Pritch had gone down the hall and I closed the door to my room and looked around. I could see Avery's room beyond, the door open, and Avery sleeping, face down, on her bed. I went in and woke her up.

She sat up immediately, blinking rather sightlessly, as if her pale eyes didn't work. "I've been asleep for hours," she said through her yawn. Then she had a good stretch. "What time is it?"

I looked at my watch. It had stopped. I shook it a little.

"You've been having sex!" she said in breathless discovery.

I just looked at her, wondering at her perception, and she gazed wide-eyed at me in return. Then she smiled.

"Good girl!" she said. "I don't blame you a bit. Pritch is really something pretty special, isn't he? Was it the first time?"

"The first time all around for me."

"Good girl," she repeated happily, and all at once I felt as if I had unwittingly been given membership in some club or other, and vaguely accompanying this feeling was the feeling that it was a club I didn't want to belong to, a nasty club.

"I'm sorry about it," I admitted.

"You are?" she asked incredulously. "Why? Because of Tim? Or wasn't it any fun?"

"None of those things." I gestured vacantly.

"You're feeling guilty and because you're afraid Tim will be terribly miffed—don't be. That's why I went off with Tim," she continued, not giving me a chance to explain. "— I wanted you to see what he was like before you two got all involved. Tim would make love to a sea gull if it had money or gave any promise of it—"

"That's an awful thing to say," I defended him.

"But it's true. Tim has decided that we can't be as poor as we look without taking any pains to cover it up, so he's fastened on me—don't tell me you didn't notice."

"I did and I didn't." Then after I said it, I realized it didn't matter, that Tim was gone; indeed he had never been there.

Slowly I told Avery about it, trying to explain to her, and to myself as I went along, how I felt. She propped herself up on an elbow, her eyes keenly following mine, taking in every word I said. I told her how I had felt about Tim at first, how it was all mixed up with how I felt about Joycie and Bart and how disappointed I was at the way I had been cut out of the heart of everything—

"Just like in *Member of the Wedding*," Avery mused. "You were little sister, Frankie—"

I shook my head. Again I was and I wasn't. It was so much more. A lot of Mother too. And now this, with

Pritch—

"But didn't you feel anything when you knew you were going to let him make out with you, all the way, that is? I did, the first time—not with Pritch, but the very first time with anybody—"

"I just wanted to," I said.

Avery sighed and put her head back on the pillow, her arms under it "You're lucky, I suppose," she said very bitterly. "I felt awful afterwards, full of shame at what had happened. But that was a long time ago."

"I feel awful too," I said, again trying to make her see. "But I don't feel 'guilty'—I don't feel full of romantic reproof because I didn't let Tim be first because I was gone on him, and not Pritch—"

"Then what?" Avery asked sharply, turning her head. "You sound as if you felt nothing. You sound the way Pritch looks afterwards—just blah, as if he had only been out ice-skating or something innocent, as if the girl didn't matter, as if she could be anybody—And he's made out with *everybody*—Lesley, Vashti, Mary Barkley, Joycie too, I think."

"I don't," I said coldly.

"You're being sentimental."

"Maybe. But it doesn't matter."

Avery studied me. "You don't know how you feel," she decided. "You probably feel a lot underneath, but now you're just numb."

"No," I shook my head. I knew it wasn't this, whatever it was, and however near the truth she was.

"You're just a kid," she said. "You'll feel differently about it when you're as old as I am. I wish I had never let one of them—"

"No," I said again emphatically. "I don't feel that kind of regret. I don't feel sorry for myself."

"Well, I do," Avery mused. "Damned sorry. I wish I had waited for the knight in shining armor."

I looked at her speculatively. Maybe she did. She looked so sad and sweet lying there; rather old-fashioned. She was a throwback to another generation, a flapper in search of a rose-covered cottage, Poor Little Glad Rag Doll. "Does Madre preach Freud at you? Did she send you to the psychos?" I asked.

"No," she said. "Madre believes in letting you grow out of it if you're a crazy mixed-up kid."

"I think she's wrong," I murmured.

"Do you?" Avery asked. "I think everybody's wrong. The parents in particular and the rest of us in general. I hate being what I am. I just plain old hate being. Don't you ever feel like that?"

I was filled with sorrow for her. "Yes," I couldn't help but lie to her. I couldn't leave her alone like this. But I couldn't go on either, though I could tell from the expectant way she looked at me that she thought I would elaborate on it.

"You and Pritch have a lot in common," she said coldly, virtually accusing me. "Neither of you feels a damned thing."

"That's not true," I said. "At least not for me. Of course I can't answer for Pritch."

"I can!" she said in anger. "I can answer for all the

Pritches—not for Tim, he's more like I am. At least I think so. The Pritch people have built-in robot souls that require no individual management, so they are left free to do anything they please, ride herd on everybody's feelings and always keep themselves intact. I'm not like that. I care about other people."

I gazed at her and wondered if she had the least idea what she was saying. It wasn't that she wasn't smart enough or perceptive enough to know—maybe she was too much of both, and this built a wall too high for the simplicity of truth to shine over. "I guess you think you're unselfish, altruistic—" I began.

"I am, to a degree," she snapped. "I can see through you, Chloe Longtree. You're just jealous and think I'm a body-snatcher, that I just reached out and took Tim away and then pretended to myself that I was trying to do you a favor because I couldn't admit I'd do a thing like that—" She bit her lip, stopped. "Don't you think that?"

"I feel dazed," I said.

Her lip curled scornfully. "I'll just bet you do, coward."

I thought about it. Was I a coward? Probably. And it was certainly true that she had succeeded in making me pity her, rather than sympathize with her, which was exchanging like for dislike.

"Go on, speak up!" she demanded in a voice very much like my mother's.

"All right, I will," I said. "I don't know what to 'think' about you although I 'feel' some very definite things. But I do know for myself that I'm sorry about all this—not just with Pritch, it went back much further, it went back to the wedding and Tim—but all this includes you."

"Okay, sage. How do you feel?"

"As if I had violated my sense of responsibility."

She gave a harsh raucous laugh. "My God! You're conscience-stricken!"

"No," I shook my head. "You don't understand. I see that now. 'Conscience-stricken' is an old meaningless term—for grandmothers—if you knew what it was all about you couldn't use it."

"I suppose the next thing you'll do is call me a neurotic?"

"That's right," I said.

She hooted with laughter. "And here I just thought I had a bad personality, a wrong attitude—"

"That's it precisely," I told her. "It makes all the difference."

"A rose by any other name," she smirked, trying to be amiable again.

I nodded. I wished her no ill. But I knew I could never make her understand. How could I when her life hadn't?

VIII

I awoke as I had gone to sleep-—feeling as if I were drowning—and for a few minutes I lay there in the big puffy bed and thought about it, as I fought my way back into life, dawning consciousness, just as the night before I had felt it squeezing from me, and I remembered a poem by Emily Dickinson that I had never realty understood, but which had some terrifically real lines in it. *After great pain a formal feeling comes…This is the hour of lead…As freezing people recollect the snow, first something, then something, then the letting go….*

I had slept like a stone, but I realized I had slept badly, as well I might have. A great sorrow settled on me, as if I had remembered that someone I loved very much had just died. And I was full of fatigue, or fanteague, it really was as I discovered in the dictionary not long ago. How could I go downstairs and face them again?

A sea of sound moved below, their voices, and in the sunny world outside my window. Things sang and it sounded happy everywhere. Their voices were lilting, full of a quality that was almost business-like; everyone was going about pleasure as if they meant it. Only I felt sad; fanteagued and finished.

I thought of what my mother had said about coming here. She was right, of course, only somehow it had all been my fault, not theirs. They were not to blame for their madness and irresponsibility. Like Topsy, they just grew, and I should have left them alone. I dragged myself up and went to look out the wide window onto the happy world.

My room faced the drive, and I could look down the stately avenue to the iron gate. I wished that at this minute I was going out of it forever. Mother quite often said that if there were any grace at all in this world people would just curl up and die after they outlived their usefulness. I felt like that; or maybe I was the one who should curl up and die....

"Good morning, you brazen hussy," Tim greeted me when I went into the sitting room where they all were.

"How shy-making!" Avery said to him. Then added to me. "Come see Madre's bust. They're having a sitting now. On the porch."

"And don't knock it over," warned The Neck. "Someone ruined the first one, and the sculptress was too upset. We never found out who it was, but I, of all people, was under suspicion."

"I didn't do it," said Blossom Nefkin in such a guilty voice that it was almost certain she had.

"Madame Polay was wild," said Avery. "She's Hungarian and redheaded and simply dreadful. You'll see. She just this instant made all of us come in, but now that you're here we have an excuse to go back and watch. Madre sits as quiet as if she were frozen, or something."

"I don't think Madame what's-her-name is any good,"

said Pritch.

"Oh, she's quite gifted," The Neck assured him.

I didn't want to go to the porch. I wanted no more of their madness, and I was hungry, I wanted breakfast. No one had mentioned breakfast.

Somewhere in the house the telephone rang, but it was ignored. It rang for some time. Finally Benda, bearing a large copper tray of Arabic design, laden with cups and a tall silver pot, came slouching into the room. She beamed at everybody, put down the tray and finally turned to me. "Is you Miss Longtree?"

"Of course she is, you silly thing," Avery told her. "Why is it you can never remember anyone's name?"

"I has too many to remember," Benda explained agreeably. Then she informed me there was a phone call waiting.

I was rather surprised. "From New York?"

"Nome, it's from East Hampton."

"I can't imagine who it is," I remarked, and followed Benda out of the room to the telephone.

A strange man's voice said, "Miss Longtree? This is Charles La Marr," and paused as if I would recognize it.

Then he repeated his name and explained he was with the ad agency for which my brother worked. "Bart phoned me last night," he said, "and asked me to get in touch with you. Apparently he couldn't reach you."

"Is he back in New York?" I asked in astonishment.

"No. He telephoned from Naples. They were flying back and should get in New York tonight." Then, his voice becoming grave, he said, "Miss Longtree, your mother arrived in Italy quite ill. They will be taking her directly from the air-port to Doctors' Hospital."

The shock spread over me and I felt as I had when I was waking up, as if I were very gradually sinking out of sight.

"I know this is very disturbing news, Miss Longtree. I'm extremely sorry."

"That's all right," I murmured.

Then he went on. He would drive me into town, would pick me up in an hour.

"What's wrong with Mother?" I asked him.

"Infectious hepatitis," he said. "I don't know if you'll be able to see her."

All I could think of was that Bart and Joyce were seeing her. Why couldn't I? There seemed nothing more to say, so I agreed to be ready in an hour and we hung up.

Briefly I stood by the phone, then slowly I went to the drawing room and looked out the window at the dried lake. Mother had never been sick. Not seriously. Of course she got lots of hangovers, but they weren't really being sick. How could she get sick in such a short time? She had flown off only two days ago. And he made it sound so serious. Was she going to die? Maybe she had died already and he was breaking the news to me piecemeal. Who was he? I tried to think, but I couldn't remember ever hearing Bart mention him. But then, Bart never talked about the people in his office. I was terrified. Maybe he wasn't from Bart's office. Maybe he was a kidnapper, and this was all part of an evil scheme. I joined the others.

"How sad-making!" Avery said, and Tim looked at me

thoughtfully for a moment. They all murmured sympathy, but somehow I knew they didn't mean it. They were concerned only with themselves, even Pritch. In a moment they were treating me as if I had already gone.

Madre came in from the porch and when she heard the news she patted my shoulder. Tears leaped from my eyes, and they all looked at me curiously. I excused myself to go upstairs and pack, though in reality I had never unpacked.

But Pritch followed me up to bring my bag. "I'm sorry, Chloe," he said, meaning it. "It's a rough deal."

I nodded and turned aside so he couldn't see me as I cried. I wanted to share my tears with no one.

I got my things together and Pritch and I went downstairs, saying nothing to each other. There seemed nothing to say. Whatever any of this had been, it was all over. My loss of virginity was as unreal as the rest. I had not come of age; whatever maturity I had reached had practically nothing to do with the events of the last crazy hours. Nothing had seemed to have weight and value since that day before the wedding—and now this, this terrible thing that was happening to my mother. "What is infectious hepatitis anyway?" I asked Pritch on the stairs.

He shook his head. "Something pretty rugged, I think," he said in a troubled voice, but added, "Maybe it's not as bad as that man made it sound. Who is he anyway? You know, I'll drive you into town if you want me to."

It was sweet of him, and I gave him a smile of gratitude, but I must have looked pretty sad and rather frightened, for he added, "Come on, Chloe, drive in with me. I really ought to leave here anyway." But I shook my head. I felt a faint stir of feeling for him, for him as *him*, but last night was gone forever.

I wondered if he would ever mention it, or try to change things between us, but there was something about his look, about his sober concern for me now, that told me with flat finality that Pritch would never be serious about me, or anybody, for that matter, simply because he had made out. Sex to him was a function that had of itself as little to do with romance and sentiment as brushing one's teeth. He was far more personal and tender with me now about my mother than he had been last night Somehow I was completely in accord with him on this, was grateful that he expected nothing from me as a result of last night.

Tim, I had decided quickly, either did not know what had gone on between me and Pritch or else was unwilling to recognize it. It would have been appalling for him, for he was as easily crushed as Avery. They were right for each other somehow. He was certainly not for me, and it struck me then that I had never really thought he was. His linking himself with me I had accepted as the foolish, flattering thing it really was. Had I seriously, for two seconds, considered a future that closely included him? My heart had turned over with vanity, not love. I had been coveted, appropriated; I had belonged to someone, and I had enjoyed the superficiality of it, its charm and grace, as pleasant as good manners, but the party was over, and I felt the same finality for Tim that I felt for the others. But this was all very vague: I was much too distraught at that moment to feel anything so objective and precise.

Waiting for Charles La Marr was very painful. I said practically nothing to the others. Somebody told me that hepatitis was a disease of the liver. Somebody else said it was not, but the pancreas, and Madre remembered that she had met Charles La Marr; that he was a rather handsome man. Blossom Nefkin and Mary Sellers then remembered him too. "He used to play tennis a great deal," Mary Sellers recollected, "with that cute little McKesson girl. Didn't he marry her?"

Madre said she thought he had, then they talked about what was happening to real estate in East Hampton, how those "New York artists" were moving in everywhere and "ruining" it; then Madre happened to remember that Madame Polay was still there, and besides my mother also was an artist of sorts, and changed the subject.

I didn't care. I was disconsolate, yet riddled with anxiety. When the telephone rang I jumped, even though it was in a far-off part of the house. The same thing happened when Parsons, the only whippet allowed in the house, had a barking fit over something he saw from the window.

"Wouldn't you like a sedative?" The Neck asked me.

I thanked her, but declined. If ever I needed to be alert, it was now. I had millions of things to think of—maybe to do, once I got back to town, for I didn't really know what the situation was. Mother might be dead, and if she was…In any case, she was terribly sick. Mother. I sat there while they chattered on, more or less forgetting me, and thought of things— things she had said, things I had always meant to ask her and hadn't, the terribly touching things she had done for us that she would be brusque and snide about if we tried to thank her for. Like the time I was sick a few years ago with an infected foot, but only for a day or so, and she had flown back from California, even though she had been having a fabulous time. And the Easter when I came downstairs and found the garden completely transformed into a sort of fairyland, full of wonderful exotic flowers and Easter eggs hidden all over it, each golden, each holding a separate present—each something I really wanted. And the way she exactly knew our tastes. The marvelous way she had been over that terrible automobile accident that had been all Bart's fault. Maybe she was a lousy mother as such, but she was a super person.

Every now and then I wiped my eyes. I was crying out of gratitude as much as sorrow. How splendid it had been to have my mother for a mother! Now and again hope would dart in, but I deliberately picked it up and put it away. It was better if I prepared myself for really bad news.

Charles La Marr arrived punctually. He came in and was introduced all around. I could see that he was making a big hit, and preoccupied as I was, I could see why. He was fascinating-looking, just to begin with, even though he was definitely an older man. I wondered just how old he was, which was rather unusual for me, for usually I don't find men of his age very interesting. He gave the appearance of youth, though he was far from looking collegiate, or dapper, or any of the things one usually associates with "youthful" older men. Rather, he looked young in the manner of a Hollywood screen star who is still playing romantic leads after ten years, but without disillusioning anybody. It wasn't that he was no-ticeably handsome, though he was far from unattractive. He had what they describe as "character" in his face, a good, well-proportioned body, and exquisite taste. He was dressed for the city, but Madison Avenue didn't scream at you.

Silently, I compared him with Bart, who, of course, is a lot younger, but the comparison was still valid, and he didn't suffer by it. He was, in short, exactly what I always thought of, in his age group, as the Beautiful People. He would never disappoint me in Sun Valley or the Riviera or Nassau. He was right. It comforted me that he was so right. As he chatted with the others, I wondered again why Bart had never men-tioned him. He was worth mentioning, and apparently they had real regard for each other, however separate they had kept their after-hours lives. This comforted me too. I was filled with acceptance of Mr. Charles La Marr. This was no kidnapper.

On that endless drive into town he was diffident, casual, solicitous, and even funny. We didn't talk much. Actually, I said practically nothing, as I had to think, but he still said some very funny things. There was one about a cloverleaf on the highway—I can't remember it—and something terribly witty about the Long Island Railroad, which he took into town every Monday in the summer. He was driving in today especially for me, I knew, though he was far too nice and intelligent to say so. The trip was as painless as possible, and when I got out of the car and thanked him I thought what marvelous eyes he had, and wonderful pepper and salt hair which he wore in a crew-cut—the only deliberately youthful thing about him. He was very kind, and sad in a way, not just because this was a sad time for a passenger in his car, but over a private sadness.

"Tell Bart to call me at any hour of the night," he said. "I want to help if I can. He did it for me."

"Oh?" I said impulsively.

"Yes. Bart was my right arm when I went through the same thing with Patsy." He didn't look directly at me. "Patsy was a wonderful girl," he added. "Bart will tell you. Good-by, Chloe. I hope you'll look in on me if you ever come up to the office. And be sure and tell Bart I'm standing by. You too. We may lick this thing yet. They know a lot more about hepatitis than they did when Patsy died."

Then he got in his car and drove away, and I knew that he *had* married the "McKesson girl," that her name had been Patsy, and that she had died.

PART THREE

I

Mother did not die, but she's going to, for it wasn't hepatitis after all, but cancer of the liver. Because she had jaundice they misdiagnosed it at the hospital in Naples.

I think Mother knew it all along, and, like an outsmarting patient in analysis, went along with the hepatitis idea just to see how far they would go before they caught themselves. Bart accused her of this, and she said, "What difference does it make? I'm going to die anyway. Does it matter if they thought I was going to die of hepatitis instead of cancer? They're all fools, and we all have to die. They do too."

To die. For weeks I said this to myself. We all have to die. "Sweet Chloe," Mother said to me when I cried—I couldn't help it—"be happy, my dear, and just don't drink too much and you'll last longer. I never found out what I was, really. That's why I drowned reality. It's so irksome not to know what one is. Maybe you'll find out. Especially if you don't drink. Do you drink?" She sat up in bed on her terribly thin elbow to ask me this. All signs of health had gone from her; only her eyes remained the same: sharp, interested, calm. And she had amazing verbal vigor; her voice sounded as it always had, though there were some days when she was too weak to talk and then saw no one.

"Yes, I more or less drink," I told her candidly. I had never been able to lie to her without misery, and I saw no need for it now.

"What has happened to you this summer?" she asked studying me. "It's none of my business, of course, but as person to person I'd like to know. I won't hold it against you," she said with a weak but wicked smile.

I shrugged. I couldn't tell her. I didn't really know; or rather, I knew all the facts, but I didn't know their dimensions. Anyway, I couldn't tell her. She was still my mother and, though softened, still somehow an enemy alien.

"Did you go off and do something unspeakable with one of those simpering young men? When I heard that you'd done precisely what I told you not to do, as soon as my back was turned, had gone to visit those Southampton madcaps, I knew I'd find you changed. You aren't a little girl any more."

I flicked my eyes at her and made no answer. How many times had I sat at a similar but stronger inquisition, one in which she strode up and down the room, declaiming, amusing herself. Then it had always seemed to me that she listened only to herself, didn't care at all, but now I wondered. What a strange mixture of people my mother was! But mostly an old *enfant terrible* and, I remembered with shock and bewilderment, a dying one.

"Chloe," my mother said in a serious, sensitive voice, "little girl." For a moment I thought she was going to reach out her hand to take mine, but then she sighed. "You and Bart," she shook her head depreciatingly. "And now Joycie. Somehow I'm responsible for you waifs."

"We aren't waifs, Mother."

"No?"

I shook my head and felt the disgusting telltale tears come up in my eyes. I loved her so. How could I tell her, show her?

"Get out the list," she said. "I just remembered Maggie Sheffield."

Ever since she had wheedled the certain facts out of the doctor, she had been making a list of people she wanted to send a form letter to. And the form letter was awful. She wanted to write to everybody she disliked, despised, disrespected, telling them exactly why, and for this purpose she had composed a general letter, already multigraphed twice, in batches of two hundred, with ample space at the bottom for her to add in each case an individual paragraph. She was constantly getting ideas for improving the letter, and I knew I would be off to the multigraphers a dozen times more, and constantly adding to the list. As I say, it was an awful letter, but it was admirable in a way. Bart would have none of it, and Joycie, when she saw the list by accident one day and found her own mother's name on it, wouldn't allow the topic to be discussed. Bart reassured her, told her the letter would never go out, of course, but I had to swear to Mother that I, personally, would see to it that it did.

All this was in August, and the doctors had told Bart Mother would be gone by then. She knew this, and took a boundless pleasure in pointing out to them that they had been wrong. I think we all took hope from it. Maybe, we hoped fancifully, she didn't have cancer after all; maybe the trouble would just go away. She kept saying she wanted to come home from the hospital. "If I have to die this season," she said, "let me do it where I please"; so Mother came home.

"Where has your social life gone to?" she asked me after she had been back about a week.

"I don't know," I told her in all honesty. I hadn't even thought about it. Outside of seeing two or three movies, getting a few telephone calls, I hadn't noticed it.

"Look, my little girl," she told me, "let me be sick. You be well. Your brother and Joyce are no better. They mope around here all the time. The other night Joyce came in to sit and brought her needlepoint. My God!"

It was true that the whole downstairs was like a hospital. It was no longer a place in which to entertain, this house that had existed for so many years for entertainment only. Altogether it had changed. And Joyce and I were like strangers, and not very friendly ones. She and Bart had the third floor to themselves—painters and plumbers and carpenters had been there for days making it into a snug, secure nest. I never went up there at all. And the downstairs, after Mother came, was another place too. The house now existed in three worlds—theirs, hers, and mine. Even mine, my own room that I had always known, the bath, the dressing room across the hall, seemed estranged, if not strange, as if the foundation of the house, and the bottom floors and the top story, had been taken away in the night. I felt stranded in the past, pushed into the future. The truth of it was I wanted to see no one.

But Mother insisted. "Ask some people in," she urged Bart. "You won't disturb me. After all, you and Joycie are newlyweds, you must do something. What will you do when I really die? Have a huge 'Thank God' party? I would, probably, but still it would be fun if life went on again here. Bart, this house was not meant to be an infirmary."

Poor Bart. Whenever she said these things he cried. Shamelessly. I don't know whether it bored my mother, or made her so sad that she had to be facetious about it in order to bear it at all. Truly I knew that she was scared to die. "I'll be nothing, little girl, nothing," she murmured to me one day when she was gazing out toward the middle of the room, wearing an expression she had worn very often since her sickness.

I longed at such moments to have some ready mother-wit to give to her, but I didn't. I was frozen, with grief, revulsion, and anxiety about the future.

"Look, Chloe," she said to me one day. "All that junk about leaving money to the Catholic Church instead of to you two is all reconsidered."

"How about the Dog and Cat Hospital?"

Irritably, she shook her head from side to side. "Dogs and cats—let them look after themselves," and then she fell into a drugged sleep.

One sleep led to another. Seldom was Mother to be seen after dinner.

Dinner all alone for the three of us was a dismal thing. Joycie, since she had gotten her third-floor precincts, was no friend of mine. Had she ever been? Sometimes I thought about it. It was as if she had died, not Mother. Even her facial expressions had changed. Very seldom did she remind me of my best friend, Joyce; most of the time this Joyce was simply my brother's wife. She never ventured down to her old haunts on the second floor, and when I met her in the den or the dining room, or Mother's room, she seemed to be only a sister-in-law, one I did not know very well. I had tried, when they first came back, and while Mother was still in the hospital, to tell her about things. Her words had been warm and interested, but her eyes had not. Afterwards, I was sure she hadn't heard a word I said: nothing about Tim, about Pritch, had penetrated. Only when I spoke about Avery did she look as if I had hit upon something familiar, however nauseous. "Oooh, how can you stand that slutty girl?" she asked.

I was livid. "How would you like it if she talked about you that way?"

"She couldn't."

"Why not? Just because you're safely married?"

Joyce gave me a funny look, but a very prim one. "I'd rather not discuss it, if you don't mind," she said. She stood up, willing to risk herself no further.

"But suppose I do?" I asked acidly.

"Well," she shrugged. "You'll just have to. I refuse to fight." She left the room, and I sat there, filled with fury. The fact that it was all impotent fury made it no better, not for anybody. In that moment I found it difficult to remember who Joyce was, who she had ever been. She was an irritating alien—another one to add to the host in the house. Doctors came and went all day; there was the day nurse, the night nurse, there were strange people doing strange things, all unknown to me, to their rooms upstairs. Apparently Joyce had ordered these. And my Bart was a shadow who flitted in and out at mealtime. He, with Joyce, disappeared after dinner. I was left alone with Mother and TV, or really just TV, for Mother read a great deal, when she wasn't under sedation because of the pain, or on the phone talking long distance to her old lovers, about whom she made no pretense now, scattered to the ends of nowhere. I was weary, useless.

Sometimes Bart let me use his car, though I didn't, of course, have a license, and I took myself for dreary drives along Bruckner Boulevard, to City Island, and once very far out on the Belt Parkway in Brooklyn where I parked, all alone, and listened to the radio. I'm a good driver, and I like to drive. Traffic is a challenge that excites me. But Mother flipped when she heard about my doing this, and after that I borrowed Bart's car on the sly. Once I took Tennie with me. There were only Tennie and Jess now. Kathleen had left of her own accord in the early summer, and there was no need for Tony. He had been Mother's chauffeur primarily, and Mother would no longer be using the car. "I'm just like I started, Miss Chloe," Tennie said mournfully on the night of our drive. "'Course now I got that no 'count Jess to hep some, but mostly I just like I started with Miss Cornelia. She was my gal and I been doing for her all her life. She mighty brave, Miss Cornelia. I know she don't want to die none. She's having too good a time."

"She always does," I said, hoping I wouldn't cry again.

"Oh, law! I reckon she don't care if she die. I think the

worse things hurts her is you, and just maybe Mr. Bart, but he seems real settled down. And Miss Joycie. She used to be 'round the house so much, but now she's a real growed-up, married lady and don't sound like herself. I had me a cousin did like that. Never would have knowed she was the same person once she got the ring en her finger. Turned out to be just as feisty and prissy—Reckon what's made Miss Joycie get so feisty?"

"Just like you said, the ring on her finger."

Tennie sighed. "Some of 'em get over it and go back to being like they was, and some don't."

"Which do you think Joycie will be?"

Tennie shook her head doubtfully. "Miss Joycie was always a sweet child. She still is some days. But she's bothering your mamma with all that grown-up acting."

"Yes," I agreed. "I'm surprised Mother still lets her come in her room." And I was surprised, for another thing that Joycie did in her new role was the Florence Nightingale bit and looking awfully Pre-Raphaelite—flowing robes and all—about it too. She really was insufferable.

It was ghastly hot, much too hot even to drive, so I moved over into the lane for the turn-off at 96th Street. We had driven almost to Connecticut, where it was slightly cooler, but the West Side Highway was jammed with cars full of people also suffering from the folly of thinking the Hudson would afford a breeze as cool as the river looked. The big neon signs lining the river on the Jersey shore were like searing torches. This was a night to look at something cool, and the river was not enough. Ships lay at berth all the way down, restless-looking as the water lapped against them. Eager to be off to cooler places, Northern Lights, snow. "I think I'll have a gin and tonic when we get home," I announced.

Tennie made a sound of mockery and disgust. "You just have yourself a limeade like you always done."

"I drink now, Tennie," I told her placidly.

"Not in Miss Cornelia's house you don't."

This was true, or almost; I hadn't had a drink in the house in all the months since Avery's, except for one night when Mother was particularly restless and got a craving for champagne. But it had made the pain so violent she announced she was "on the wagon for the duration."

Mother was sitting propped up in bed, her hair in a pony tail, when I got home. She said she was feeling exceptionally well, had just given Joyce and Bart a going over.

I smiled. "Where are they? Upstairs?"

"No. Some friend of Bart's called and they went out for a change. The friend was very amusing, asked me to come along."

"I'm surprised you didn't."

"I'm rather surprised I didn't too. The friend was quite attractive. You know him, by the way. He's the one who brought you back alive from the Cowles' wilds—Mr. La Marr."

"Where did they go?" I asked, interested now.

"To the Blue Angel."

I guess I looked wistful because she said, "Too bad you weren't here. You could have gone with them."

I was stunned, and in a way saddened. This was the last

link, and she had willingly, cheerfully broken it. I was permanently parted from little girlhood. "Does that mean you give me permission to go out to places like that?"

She laughed uneasily. "Why not? You go anyway, don't you? I know what you do, Chloe. Oh, I know you've been dutifully sitting by my side, lodged like a lump of clay, all summer. But you were tearing around those few days I was gone—especially with Avery Stafford."

"Who told you I was 'tearing around'?"

"A gossip columnist."

"Probably by the name of Joyce."

"No, it wasn't Joyce. I'll show you the clipping. A kind friend sent it to me a few days ago. Had been saving it, apparently; though, mind you, Joyce would have brought it to my attention if she had seen it. She's brought other things to my attention. She's under the impression that we are grownups together. I can't think why. I'm not nearly so adult as she is these days."

"I hate her," I said.

"Don't sound so petulant," Mother told me. "Besides, you don't hate her at all. Joyce will be restored to you. Just you wait. But for the moment I think it would be a good thing if you let her have her head and stopped tagging after her and Bart all of the time."

"You just suggested yourself that I might have gone out with them tonight."

"That's not tagging after. I'm talking about here in the house. You must learn to stop leaning on people. Which brings us up to the question of school this fall. I think you've outgrown Chalmers. Why don't you write your Aunt Maude and have her look around for something over there?"

I made a face. "I may not go back to school any more."

"What do you propose doing instead?"

"I think I'll take a course or something and get a job."

"Oh, Chloe!" She sighed irritably. "You're making me very tired."

And cross, I almost added spitefully. I stood up coldly.

"No contrition?" she asked with a sort of malicious smile.

"No contrition."

"Well, go then. You've no idea how trying it is to be a captive audience."

I gave her a long look. "I rather think I do," I said.

As I went out of her door I heard Joycie and Bart coming in downstairs through the kitchen. I went down to join them, taking the steps two at a time.

Suddenly I felt very giddy and playful. I wanted to tease something.

Joycie was looking in the fridge, poking around, probably planning a tidy little midnight meal. Housewifely.

"Hello, Mole," Bart said. "Where did you get that peasant outfit?"

"In the garment district," I tossed back at him.

"You have clothes I like better," Joycie commented.

"You haven't," I answered, and Bart gave me a sharp glance.

"Now, now, bitches," he said, "no tearing up the carpet."

"Charles La Marr is nice," Joyce said to him, ignoring my presence. "I think it would amuse your mother to ask him around for drinks or something."

"Sure. Why not?"

II

Charles La Marr was asked to dinner on a Thursday. I know, because it was the only thing in my engagement book for that whole period. After that I just lost track.

How do these things happen? I don't know. You find someone interesting, then fascinating, then irresistible. Then you say to yourself, "Am I falling in love with him?" And you answer, "No, of course not. It's just that I like him a lot, like to be with him, more than anybody else." And before you know it you *are* with nobody else. And there it is.

It didn't really start with dinner, though it almost did. It was one of those dinners where everything was completely right. All the right things were said, brilliantly right and spontaneous, as if we were all geniuses, and it just built and built, spiraled upward. Bart was divine, Mother was superb, and Joyce and I giggled together like fiends. Charles La Marr—indescribable. He was just out of this world. Blue sky.

Mother felt so well that she got all gussied up and came downstairs for awhile, for the first course. I wore something Mother said at first she wouldn't be caught dead in, but then changed her mind about, and even Joyce said, "You look smashing," as we were going downstairs. The whole night was like that: perfect.

I think Charles made it that way; he and Mother glanced off each other like refracted light, but for once she didn't upstage anybody. But isn't it funny that afterwards, after one of those rare marvelous encounters, you can't remember anything specifically? I can't remember one enchanted word, and to say we talked about such and such renders it as flat as a wonderful dream told the next day. The magic should be left alone, untouched. It spoils it to examine it.

I know I felt this way about Charles that night when I went to bed. I wanted to hold my mind, stop it, as if it were breath, so thoughts wouldn't creep in to tarnish it. I didn't even want to put it into consciousness that I had had eyes for no one else, as they say. Indeed, it was as if I had no eyes at all, only Charles'. A brilliant ravishing world had opened up for me through his eyes, and as he spun out his myth, like a tinsel charm, I experienced all of the emotions with him, terrible rending tenderness, the giddiest of lofty heights, the endless placidity and safety of grassy plains.

I say his "myth," when what I really mean is his "story," to put it in less exotic terms, and I make it seem unreal, and as if he were talking just to me. But the truth was, he was charming us all.

Charles had grown up in the wonderful years, or at least they sounded more wonderful than any we have now, and of course he had been everywhere that was exciting or chic to go, spoke eight languages, including Urdu and an obscure dialect of Arabic, and knew, it seemed, everything on earth. Even Mother was impressed and she remarked later that it was a relief to meet someone totally saturated with aware-ness, dipped in worldliness as if it were a rich purple dye.

It never occurred to me that night Charles had taken more than passing pleasurable notice of me. He and Mother were such obviously kindred spirits that I thought he had been absorbed, delighted only in her, and felt genuine regret that nothing could ever come of it. There wasn't even time or opportunity for friendship.

So that no matter how gone I knew I was, I couldn't be-lieve it when Bart came home from his office the next day and said, "Chloe, do you know what 'captivating' means?" and before I could answer, added, "Because if you don't, you'd better look it up. That's what I hear you are. You've really made it, kid. Guess we'll have to stop calling you 'Mole' and 'little girl' and doll names. You won't have to come out now. We can have all that money—you're already out."

"Stop it. I don't like it," Mother snapped at him. At this he whooped with laughter.

"Cornelia!" he blasted at her. "You're jealous!"

Sometimes it was hard to remember Mother was sick; hard for her too. "You're an ass," she told him. Me she ad-vised, "Now don't go getting your head turned just because a middle-aged charmer has decided you're a juicy morsel. I won't have it. People should stay in their own class and their own age group."

Both Bart and I snickered at this sage pomposity, for Mother had scarcely done either.

"I won't have you running around town with him," she warned, "getting 'bombed' every night, as you call it 'Living furiously,' or whatever else you call it."

"'Living it up,'" I corrected her. "Anyway, he hasn't asked me yet."

"He won't," Bart predicted. "He was simply admiring you. I don't think Charlie would go for young stuff."

"What a vulgar expression!" Mother said.

"I like him," I said.

"Forget about it," Joycie advised, joining in on this for the first time.

"Come off it, Joyce," Bart remonstrated. "Chloe's no fool."

But I knew I just might be. It was too soon to tell. I stored it all up in the back of my mind; I would think about it.

I had a lot of time to think, just then, as it happened. It was the beginning of September, and still terribly hot. Joyce spent three weeks in Connecticut, with Bart up only for weekends, and I stayed in town. Pretty much alone. Once I got blasted on aquavit with Portia, that beast, when she came to town with her parents for three days; guess where they stayed: the Piccadilly. Then she was gone—and I hadn't dug up a single date for her, though we did play tennis one day— and there wasn't anybody. I had called Avery several times, but there was never any answer. And Joyce's mother had asked me up there, but somehow I didn't go. Maybe it was because I had found out Joyce was going to have a baby, and even with all ten fingers, nine didn't really work. Eight did, much better. I didn't talk to Bart about it—he always seemed to be high, and very far away, when I saw him.

About the middle of the month we had a blow. Mother

had been getting progressively worse, at home, for all her show of spirit, and had to go back to the hospital. To Memorial this time, the cancer place, but that was done as a gesture, for it was really hopeless. Doctors always believe in keeping up hope, for some reason. Mother was dead set against it when she found out. "Why can't I die at home? There's nothing to be done for me in the hospital."

Then the doctor reminded her, as tactfully as possible, that there were other people to consider too. Not only would she be more comfortable at Memorial, and receive better-organized if not superior care, but she would be freeing us to live our own lives as we must inevitably do.

"I deserved that," she murmured and Bart and I both broke down and cried like babies.

This was my first lesson in the cruelty, the harshness and bitterness, of implacable facts. Thank God there are very few such moments in life—people couldn't stand it at all if there were more. As T. S. Eliot says, there is only birth, and copulation, and death. Two are painful, two are long, and only the one in the middle is short and sweet. It is not worth it, probably, yet it causes the other two. An insoluble riddle. And now Mother was on the third lap, the hardest of all. Having been brought forth into life, she was being put from it, as surely as if the physicians who healeth not had, in their failure, straightened her clenched, fighting hands, pulled them straight at her sides, and said: "Now take a deep breath and go! Don't bother us any more."

Mother was consigned to the hospital to die, and though she did not go about it dutifully, as prescribed, she lost ground.

"Why, why do I have to die?" She mourned aloud one day. Tennie was sitting beside her too.

"'Cause you can't live, Miss Cornelia," she told her placidly, and I thought it was the wisest thing I'd ever heard.

It wasn't long after that that she began to lapse into a coma. The doctors thought perhaps it had reached the brain….How can I say how terrible it was, still is? Only sometimes she is better than others. Sometimes she goes for weeks without a coma. But, as Bart remarked, what difference does it make?

But just after they took her back to the hospital, she got up her fighting spirit and was ferocious for a time; just wonderful. We perked up as a result. It was sometime in this period that I saw Charles La Marr again.

There were lots of papers and things for me to sign, along with Bart—Mother was being very thorough—and Bart suggested that we go down to the lawyer's office together and then have lunch. I was glad, thinking maybe I'd be able to talk to him this time. We went to the Drake, because it is not far from Bart's office, but he didn't tell me until we got there that Charles La Marr was joining us.

Just as he was telling me, Charles came in, wearing a magnificent suit that he told Bart he had bought in Italy, when Bart asked.

"How's your mother?" he asked us, steering me forward to our table. Then, because I hesitated, he said, "I suppose people should really stop asking you that."

I nodded and felt like crying. I mostly felt like crying these days. Then he went on about Mother, quietly, with deftness and charm, then the subject was dropped.

"How would the Longtrees like to spend Thanksgiving in East Hampton?" he asked. "I've decided it is a healthy, sane and rather grand holiday to observe. There would be just us, and maybe two or three others. We would sort of dig in."

I wondered, almost jealously, even then, about the two or three others as I saw Bart considering the question. But of course he would accept; that many weeks from now there was sure to be nothing to keep us at home. Bart had calculated that way too and said we would love to come.

"I'm afraid I don't know any frisky youngsters," he said to me with a smile, "but we can act young."

It was the first awkward, defensive thing I had heard him say. There was no answer to it, really, so I made a deprecating gesture and smiled. He couldn't be perfect; I had no right to expect it.

Bart started on his second martini. He certainly seemed to be knocking them back these days. "Let's not have a wet lunch," he remarked, as if to himself. "At least not you, Mole. Eat something solid."

Charles grinned at him and fingered the stem of his glass. He didn't seem to drink much; his glass was still nearly full, so Bart's admonition was meant purely for the family.

Then Charles and Bart talked about accounts for a while. I was fascinated. I had never heard Bart talk shop before. He's such a strange guy; and his life is so completely compartmentalized—the way Mother always meant hers to be, and stoutly insisted it was, though it was no more so than the Emperor's New Clothes. But Bart's really is. I think he learned from her how to make it so. Another thing I regretted: that I hadn't known Mother as long as he.

Bart ordered another martini and Charles ordered lunch. When Bart went to the men's room, Charles said: "Does Bart get stiff at home?"

I shook my head loyally, rather resenting the question. But then I realized that Charles' interest sprang from concern. "It won't make your mother well," he told me. "And don't you start it either."

I suppose I looked guilty, even though I wasn't, really. "Why didn't we meet you before last summer?" I asked rather insultingly, as if I were sure there was some excellent, however disreputable, reason for not having done so.

"Well, let me see," he said. "First of all, Patsy, that was my wife, and I lived on Majorca for several years. Then we came back here. And then I came to the agency last fall and Patsy died. And I wasn't there for a few months. Then I went back, because I hadn't sold my interest, though I had rather planned to. I went back, I suppose, to fill the time. And you were probably at school then, weren't you?"

"Yes," I murmured, chastened. "And Mother was in Europe." And Father was in Heaven, and what business was it of mine where he was, or why we hadn't met him?

"I expect you'll be coming out next year, won't you?" he asked genially.

I pondered. "That was the plan," I said at last, "but of course since Mother is going to die it sort of changes things."

"Oh, I don't know," he replied speculatively. Then, "What are you going to do when you grow up, Chloe?"

"Do my best," I told him with a smile. "That probably sounds flip and silly," I added rather apologetically. After all, he was older. "But I mean it."

"Forgiven," he smiled. Then Bart came back. He was rather bombed.

"Forgive me if I don't eat," he said sitting down. "I feel very liquid today."

Neither Charles La Marr nor I said a word. The food had arrived, and I began to contemplate it, then eat it.

Bart seemed very preoccupied with the stem of his glass, and his face was now rather flushed. Did he, of all people, have a drink "problem," and if so, since when? Then the waiter came over. Bart had a phone call.

"It's probably the office," he told us, excusing himself.

"We have a new and very touchy client," Charles told me. The small lines around his eyes were deeply drawn, giving him a worried look. I wondered if he was having doubts about Bart's ability to handle it.

"Bart has always drunk very well," I felt moved to assure him.

"Really?" Charles replied absently, not convinced.

"Is Bart—?" I paused. I had been about to ask if Bart was about to flip or something, and then decided it was not only too personal, but rude in a way. Undoubtedly, Charles La Marr thought of me as demure. Sweetheart roses, sweet sixteen. Let him think it. I was glad I looked it that day, glad I looked well, though of course if I had dressed for anyone I had dressed for the lawyer. Mother was always fond of recommending that a woman should for every man she planned to meet, whether it was the president or the stable boy; that way it was impossible to go wrong. However, Mother and Mother's axioms had always been two different things. I had decided a long time ago I wouldn't be that way; the way to avoid it was to be less reckless. Then Pritch jumped into my mind. I had been as reckless that night as Mother ever was....

"What were you about to say?" Charles asked. I realized he had been waiting for me to finish my question.

I was saved from answering because Bart came back, somewhat recovered. "The appointment has been switched," he told Charles and added, to me, "Sorry Mole, but I have to get right back. Why don't you come back to the office when you've finished? I won't be involved for more than a half-hour or so."

I said I would, and then Bart gave Charles a peculiar look and said with a brotherly laugh, "Don't let Chloe get out of hand, Charlie."

It was an astonishing thing for him to have said, and before I could offer any protest, or ask him to "define his terms," as he was fond of saying, he had gone.

Charles and I continued our lunch in silence, and when the menu was handed to us to order dessert, I wondered if I were boring him. I felt not just naive and gauche, sitting there with this handsome older man, but very little-girl, very straw-hat-and-streamers little girl, and as if my feet didn't quite reach the floor. Why was I feeling like this?

The waiter gave me a benign smile, confirming my youth.

"I will have a chocolate parfait," I told Charles coldly, ignoring the waiter. I knew my clothes were grownup enough. Was my face so bland and unworldly as all that? Avery Stafford wouldn't have had this trouble.

After the dessert arrived, while Charles was sipping his coffee, he said, "You have the most appealing face. I was noticing it all through lunch. It changes all the time. Not just in expression, the way most faces do, but aesthetically, as if it were being played on by soft colored lights. Sometimes you look years older than you are, and then the next minute years younger."

"Do I ever look my age?"

"I don't really know what your age is," Charles said. "That was one of the reasons I asked if you were planning to come out next year—just a shot in the dark."

"So now you know how old I am from my answer."

"Generally."

I mused about it for a moment. In two months I would be seventeen. Seventeen! It seemed incredible. Last year at this time I had been fifteen. "Last year" as I thought of it was last generation, and two years before that was impossible. It was antique, and I was, as I remembered myself then, a sort of poignant china doll like something from the nineteenth century. I remembered a doll I had had, one Mother had bought at an antique shop because she liked it—not because she thought I would—and she had named it "Hitty," after a Rachel Field book I remembered she read to me when I was little. She had liked that too. I had been very jealous of Hitty, my doll, just as I had been very jealous, in a much less defined way, of the book when she had read it. And now a part of me was Hitty, poignant, nostalgic, discarded in the attic, waiting to be rediscovered.

I made a face at my dessert. "I can't finish it," I told Charles. "It's too rich."

He laughed easily, somewhat amused. "Grown-up girls usually like all that goo."

I suppose I looked at him rather resentfully; it sounded suspiciously like he was making fun of me. "I still like junky desserts," he said. "If you won't finish it, I will."

As I pushed the parfait over to him I liked him very much again. I watched the way he ate it: lovingly, caressingly, as if every bite were silky and delicious. It made me laugh.

"You think I'm crazy, don't you?" he asked in mock sternness.

"Sort of," I admitted. Impulsively I wanted to say too that he was crazy in such a nice way—not like Bart or my mother, who were nearly always funny. But he seemed more compatible, comfortable, like someone my age. It was funny. I couldn't quite dig him, or the peculiar way he made me feel, as if he were three or four people at once, all nicely melded together so he was really one. He was really all-around, like the honor they confer in school, one which I held in complete awe and could never hope to win; well-wrought. I wondered if he had had a good childhood too. Everything about him seemed so contented, smooth-running. "Have you always been this way?"

"What way?" he asked, quite understandably.

"Sort of—" I gestured. "Well. I don't know how to put

it—glad, sort of."

"No," he said flatly. "If 'miserable' meant anything any more, I'd say that it described a big hunk of the time for me."

I looked astonished. "But why?"

"Misery is a state of disgrace just as contentment is a state of grace," he said lightly, smiling at me. "I think you know exactly what I mean, Chloe, and you just want something to gauge your own feelings by—not that I mind, my dear; we all do it. But don't you move from 'states' of malcontent into areas of contentment? Anyway, you've had a good, strict guide. I can tell that Cornelia Longtree knows her business. She's not ever going to let you let yourself be really unhappy, or silly, or go through any of the stages kids sometimes have to wrestle with."

"Oh, don't you think so!" I said bitterly, thinking his benign, smug fatherly attitude absolutely repulsive. "I don't know what kind of life your parents led you, but I can certainly tell you about mine. It hasn't been the prettiest thing in creation."

"Prettiness...is that what's important?"

I was furious. He and his adult condescension. "You don't know everything," I said angrily, "just because you're grown up and can look back on it and draw your own conclusions about this and that. And for that matter, I *don't* know 'exactly' what you mean about states of grace, disgrace or anything."

Stormily I began to tell him a thing or two, pouring it out—about Mother, how Father had died before I was born. About those years with Aunt Maude, which I could barely remember because I could barely bear to remember them, about how Bart had stood by, then Joycie. Then there I was telling him all the rest, my voice died down like an angry sea grown calm, telling him about the wedding, how things had hurt me. About how funny and mixed up it all was with people like Avery and Tim, then Portia, my roommate, who seemed like a little child, and here I was, in the midst of it all, and now Mother was going to die. Go off and leave me, as if out of perversity.

"She can't help it," he said gently, with great tenderness. Then his fingers closed over mine, and he began to tell me about his mother, how she had died when he was a sophomore at Princeton and what his father had done to him. It was awful. How could people *do* things like that to other people? Charles had had to go to work as a deliveryman for a milk company because it had still been the Depression, when he finished working his way through college, and all his friends looked down on him. Then his father died and Charles and his new stepmother had this awful fight in court about the will, a fight that dragged on for years.

"When I finally won it and got the money," he said, "I realized I didn't want it any more. Not for the things I had wanted it for. They were all gone, those things, and those people, and I was suddenly alone with my money, like a shipwrecked sailor on a desert island with all the cargo washed up along with him. All the beautiful magic of money and childhood was gone, along with the anger against my father, which had probably replaced it, so I just left the money alone for a long time."

"You left it alone?"

"Yes. After the first spree. I bought myself a fancy long-nosed car, and lots of clothes, and threw away several thousand dollars in night clubs. Then I stopped. The magic was dead, and I left the money alone."

"What happened?"

"Like Topsy, it just grew," he said with a smile. "Till I started to travel and found out what to do with it."

His hand and mine were together all of this time, and then he said, "Hey! It's awfully late. Maybe we ought to go back to the office?"

I suppose because his statement had turned up at the end, like a question mark, I looked reluctant. Anyway, he laughed at me.

"No," he said. "I think it's much more important that we go to the Central Park Zoo, don't you?"

I nodded, not trusting myself in my explosion of sudden ecstasy, to answer.

Out on the street, while we were waiting for a cab, he turned to me, his face very serious. "Chloe," he said. "Don't mind about Pritch or all those other things you told me. Stay as you are. You're one of the best."

"No," I shook my head, barely able yet to speak.

"You are. You say all the right things."

He looked at me as if he were going to kiss me. I wanted him to—desperately.

III

And Central Park was just nothing. It might have been the moon, the Sahara, or the deep blue sea for all I knew. I went into ecstasy over the seals, I loved the sad yak, adored the raccoons and wanted to mother the hyena—or in other words I adored Charles and took out the splendor of my love on the dumb animals I was hardly aware of. I had one thing and one thing only in the back of my mind.

"Patsy was your age when I met her," he told me. Then he added with a little laugh, "Patsy was much too young for me—I thought." Then he fell silent, musing about Patsy, because she hadn't been too young for anybody; she had been old enough to die.

Adroitly, I suppose, I led the conversation around to art, to painting and sculpture, and to Mother's. Charles said he had seen one of her shows. He told me which one and I told him it was terrible.

"Oh, no," he said. "Your mother lacks technique, but she doesn't lack imagination and ability. Whom did she study painting with? Why didn't she really learn the fundamentals?"

I told him that she thought she had, and that Leger had been her last teacher—a long time ago.

He shook his head. "It's all wrong for her. She comes out Kaethe Kollwitz. Instead she should do something fine—I mean very fine lines and all that—draftsmanship would have suited her. What did she do during the war?"

"Which war?" I asked.

This made him laugh. "I forgot," he said. "To you the Second World War is what the first was to Patsy—not that I was around for much of the first one either. But do you realize, Chloe, that your mother was a grown girl when that war came along, and that I was almost ready for school then? That's how old I am."

Charles suggested that we have a hot dog and a Coke on the terrace, but I shook my head. "How about the St. Moritz across the street then?" he said, and to this I agreed.

As he guided me over, waiting until the traffic abated, I wanted a drink terribly. I needed one if I was going to do what I had to do. I wondered if he needed a drink.

My blood sang when he touched me. How can I describe it? How can I describe it when I can't really remember a single word he ever said, as he said it, that is. But I can say how I felt, how it was when he looked at me. His eyes were so warm, so intelligent, so tender that they were like a hand taking my hand, and the merest touch of him was something so exquisite that I could hardly bare to breathe. Our lives, as far as I was concerned, had not just crossed, in these few short hours, but fused. Mine was inextricably, irrevocably, eternally paced with his, part of Princeton, part of Biarritz, even part of Patsy, for he had told me about her too.

"You're like Patsy," I remember he said when we were

sitting outside the St. Moritz having our drinks. "You have her sky eyes—always blue, always serene when there is serenity, but always serious. The sky has great character, you know. All you have to know about life you can find in the sky."

I gazed at him thinking he had the most intelligent, the most hurt eyes I ever saw.

I closed my eyes for a second, for I hadn't stopped looking at him since we sat down, and when I opened them he was still there, as he was. Maybe, as he said, he was ancient, part of a world that was too remote to recapture—the Second World War was really as much as I could manage—but he did not seem so to me. The few lines in his face, and you couldn't call them lines—they were accentuations of features—had no time value. It just seemed a miracle that he could sit there and talk about something so impossible as the First World War. "I was five when the war ended," I said.

"Which war? Oh. Yes. You would have been. The Second World War. You were born in 1940. 1940…funny…in 1940 I had a house on Sixty-third Street and I had just asked Patsy to marry me…."

"Did she?"

"Yes, and I went off to something called the European Theater and was a major in the Army. Patsy stayed in the house. We sold it when I got back. As a matter of fact, Patsy had a painting by your mother. She bought it at an exhibition out in East Hampton the summer we were engaged. It was called, 'Kiki rejects Man Ray, as well as Ernest Hemingway,' and there wasn't a discernible soul in it. I think she bought it for the title."

"Do you still have it?"

He shook his head. "I gave Patsy's family all that was left of Patsy—materially, that is. What she really left I couldn't give anybody. She wasn't an easy person to forget."

"Do you really remember things—I mean, what she said on such and such an occasion, what she wore, what she thought about herself?"

"I think so," he nodded gravely. "I like to think so."

I wondered if I would keep these things about Mother. I wondered if anybody ever could. My memory, my observation, isn't bad, but still I know that streets I have walked on a thousand times hold the most inconsequential secrets that I would like to have, just to *have* them, and don't.

The afternoon had saddened somehow, but softly, softly. The sky itself was like a mood, neither blue nor gray, but pensive. It stood over Central Park as if it were a visitor. And the sky in New York is a visitor. It comes, it seems, to serve a purpose, as a theatrical backdrop is composed or summoned or fetched; it is there because that extra something is needed for an effect, but it isn't itself any more—it isn't the sky at Joyce's in Connecticut. Joyce! Bart! Mother! Most of all Mother! I had completely shed them this afternoon. My mind rapidly ticked over the plans it had conceived; yes, they were inconceivable: I had to get home. I stood up. "Charles," I said, "I'm afraid it's late and Bart will wonder anyhow why I didn't come back to the office."

"Sit down," he restrained me, holding my hand. "I'll telephone him. Anyway, I was wondering if, perhaps, you could show me some of your mother's pictures. I think I'd like to buy one. And it might make her happy."

"It would make her delirious," I said, and was positively overcome. He was better than a mind reader. All afternoon, in the back of my mind, I had been contriving a scheme to get him up to Mother's studio. "Why don't we go up to Mother's studio?" I said. I had a key, as did Bart, but we had it not for use but for precautionary measures. Before Mother got sick neither Bart nor I would have dreamed of going there except when asked, or to close the windows when it suddenly rained, or to ship her a picture when she was in Europe and had, as she said, "a live one" who wanted to buy something of hers.

Now, however, things were different. They really were. It was hers still, but it was as if it were part of my inheritance. Why did I feel this way? I was ashamed and guilty over it. Maybe I would be trespassing on sacred ground if I went there with Charles. But he had gone to telephone. Anyway, she *would* like it if he bought something of hers.

There was no talk about it, we simply got into a cab. It wasn't far. Then it was three flights up. The room was musty, sad, too hot, in this Indian-summer weather. I threw open the French windows, then Charles helped me with the sky-light, and then we went to bed.

It was all my fault. I did it all by myself. There on Mother's studio couch. He sat down beside me, and took my hand. I think he took it because it was comfortable for him to take it: he took it out of friendship, a friend takes a friend. And then I kissed him. I put my face on his, my arms around him, and kissed him. At first he responded as Bart would have done. Then it was something else: it became a real kiss, a soft kiss of compassion and wonderment. Then it changed again, and he was kissing me as no one had ever kissed me.

They call it soul kissing, and now I know what they really mean. When you mean it, and it is a soul kiss it goes to your soul: it encompasses everything, all you are, were, ever hope to be. "I'm too old for you, Chloe," he kept murmuring over and over, "much too old," but all the time he was kissing me, more and more. He only took time out to say this, putting his hands under my chin, not really looking at me, kissing me instead. Then he stood up. "It's dark"' he said, "and I must be out of my mind." He shook his head.

I didn't say a word. There wasn't a word to say. I simply stood up and kissed him. As he kissed me back, he moaned, sort of. Then we were back on Mother's couch, and I knew somehow, no matter what else, that for me the most important thing on earth was to go to bed with Charles La Marr.

He took me as if I would break, gently, but strongly, protectively. It was nothing like it had been with Pritch. I felt as if I were coming apart; I was completely liquid, disjointed, and ecstasy had taken possession of my body.

"Darling," Charles whispered. "Darling, darling." He smoothed my hair. "What is this mad thing that has possessed us?"

I shook my head, firmly, many times, from side to side. I had never felt so sane in my life. I was way beyond speech. That form of communication was nothing, less than nothing. I kissed him.

After we got up, Charles called Bart at home. Bart told

him to come to dinner. Charles declined, saying he had another engagement.

I suppose I was hurt; certainly, I was disappointed. He came over to me as I stood in my slip and put a hand gently under each of my elbows. He kissed my nose. "I'm not going to do it again, Chloe," he said in a low endearing voice, but one that meant what it said.

"What?" I asked, knowing, but wanting him to say.

"Anything, anything at all," he said, and released my elbows.

"Charles—!" I cried. But all I had, by way of argument, as recourse from what was about to happen, was that cry. He looked kindly in my protesting face and shook his head.

"No, little girl," he said. "Just no."

"Why, why?" I demanded sharply.

"The answer is in a sealed envelope, to be opened ten years from now," he told me, and added, "an answer you will have written yourself."

All this time, maddeningly, calmly, he was dressing. I wished, at that moment, that I thought it would help to cry. But for him the afternoon, the interlude was over, and tears would be as unreal to him as I had seemingly become.

"Which picture should I buy?" I realized he was saying, realized that he was actually walking around the studio gazing thoughtfully at the canvases on the wall.

I wanted to shriek. "Why don't you buy that long thin one over there?" I asked, my voice shaking, my heart stiff with irony, for it was supposedly a picture of me—not a portrait exactly, but a nasty thing she had done one night off the top of her head, when she was furious at me. I was about ten; I didn't look at all like me, but I was dragging my doll Hitty by one antique and risky leg, and Hitty looked like Hitty. It was a good picture. Charles frowned at it. "I'm not sure I really want it," he said.

I held my breath.

We went out, properly dressed, into the still-warm night air. He had the picture under his arm, and I had a check in my purse for the amount Mother had scrawled on the back of the painting as its price. I felt neither triumphant nor defiant.

"You hungry?" asked Charles.

I didn't feel that either.

Traffic was heavy. The after-dinner theater-going crowd had taken all the taxis in the vicinity. Tourists were spreading over the city like ectoplasm, taking it over. Let them have it, I thought. All that mattered, suddenly, was home, and going down in the kitchen to talk to Tennie. And maybe Jess would take us both for a ride in Mother's car. I wanted to be, as Tennie called it, "with homefolks"; this night was like being stranded on Christmas Eve in Nebraska. Why?

I looked at Charles, so remotely near, so aloofly part of me, and I hated myself. I hated, hated, hated myself! I felt like Avery. Avery! I would call her as soon as I got home, and I would shout at her, "This is the Beast! And the Beast is full of guilt!" I would. And I wouldn't care whether she understood or not—I would understand, because I understood morality, junior and senior grade.

"Are you high, Chloe?" Charles asked me. "Would you

like to have dinner out and then go home? I don't have anything particularly to do except catch a train."

The misery apparent in the eyes I turned on him must
have touched off something, corresponded to those myriad
degrees of misery of which he had told me he was master; I
didn't mean it to be. It was my own private brand; not com-
parable to his. In fact, I didn't want him any more. I wanted
the small mole-cell of hurt into which I had nestled myself,
and I wanted no intruders inside—not even visitors, semi-
well-informed ones. I wanted me to me. I guess I shuddered
as he touched me.

"You know, Chloe," he said quietly, "if you were ten
years older I'd tell you, without conscience or conflict, how
much I think I might be in love with you. And a little while
later, after we had gotten to know each other, even if I didn't
like all I got to know, I'm certain I'd ask you to marry me.
But it's ten years too soon—or too late."

I looked at him in complete wonderment. He made me
feel like a fairy princess, one who the day before had been a
mere mortal, someone sewing in the kitchen, tending fires.
There was nothing to say to him. He towered there, his face
warm, full of glow, his hand in mine, looking neither anxious
nor troubled. "Take me home," I said.

"All right," he agreed, and again turned back to the rapid,
stitching traffic that edged the side streets, flowed into the
middle, creating an unstopping and unintelligible design of
light and color. Again and again he signaled cabs. Nothing
stopped. We stood there, suspended in that realm of complete unreality called "waiting," thinking no thoughts, feeling

no fierce pulls of emotion—not anger, not exasperation, not love—just waiting, our eyes lighting only as the tops of the cabs lighted, as if they were fireflies to be copped by the nearest trapper with a mason jar. And when we got one, we both felt so tired, we could just have stopped moving then and there, and the driver could have driven us round and round while we remained in a trance of exhaustion. But Charles had given my address, and we were going there.

Vaguely, far-off, I longed for the touch of him—not so much the touch of him, but human contact. His hand. I longed for it so much that I didn't have anything left over with which to formulate thoughts to be spoken. Then he took my hand. "Aren't you hungry?" I asked somewhat dreamily.

"Chloe," he murmured. "You girls—you—you don't know what you are."

"What are we?"

"Nectar, aphrodisiac, T.N.T., the gas chamber, heaven in hell and hell in heaven."

"You sound as if you go to every deb party going."

He laughed heartily at that. Then he laughed raucously. He laughed a great deal more in an even more disturbing way. I decided he was drunk, and when we reached the house and I asked him in, in the most perfunctory way, and he shook his head, I by no means insisted.

"Stay as you are, little wild girl," was the last thing he said. He squeezed my hand and was gone down the steps.

IV

"Chloe," Mother's voice came over the telephone, alert and full of impatient authority, "I'm coming home today, and I want to talk to you as soon as possible."

I listened with amazement. I felt as if she were escaping from the madhouse, for I knew home was no place for her. Still, it was her house. The best I could do was alert everybody, see that things here were running as well as they could be. I called her doctor. He said, yes, he knew she was on her way—determined. How could you blame her, even after that lecture they had given her?

I think I was standing in the den. Anyway, I broke down and cried. And cried and cried. It seemed no more real or necessary than a traffic accident, a fire, a flood, an act of God....

God...I looked up. How long had it been since the thought of God had come to me? Pritch, way last summer, had talked about Him some, but it had seemed funny. And of course my mother didn't believe, and Bart, though he had been christened, as I had, to humor somebody in the family, had no more conception of Christianity than an infant Watusi. We lived in a so-called "Christian society," but what was that? I had no one to turn to, spiritually or otherwise. I had no one, no one, no one! I was pounding my fists on the den couch then, I think, and somehow remembering to stifle my sobs because of the servants.

Poor Tennie had it bad enough, and Jess had eyes that positively haunted me. Everyone had been in mourning for months. Why didn't she go on and get it over with? It was another mean, cruel trick, this slow dying of hers. Longer than Isolde. I sniffled and choked, lying there, on my own grieved agony on my own grieved joke.

There was no one I could turn to. Bart and Joyce were absorbed in their own problems. What was it about being pregnant, having a wife who was pregnant, that made you so *exclusive*? I had never really understood what had happened, with them. Had Bart really loved Joyce, or just wanted to sleep with her? It was a question particularly near, as they say, to personal experience, for though I was not pregnant with a baby by Charles La Marr, I was, unaccountably, perhaps, and certainly foolishly, taken up. And yet I hadn't laid eyes on him in a whole month. True to his word, he had withdrawn, and with such discretion that even Bart found no reason to wonder what had happened.

But he had ruined me. In that month, it wasn't that Mother was so sick—that was true, and bad enough, but there were many nights at the TV set when she had declined to have me at the hospital and when I had declined the company of Kermit Overall and Freddie Wayne and Conger Newton and I don't know who all, that I had known in dancing class or somewhere, and it seemed that *everybody* was in town, and having a wonderful time. And I always said no, usually because of Mother, but even they knew it was a lie. Some of their mothers knew her, knew that the infantile devotion was a myth. To turn them down made me unhappier, if anything. But oh, oh, how well I knew them! Weenie weenie weenies. The littlest Yalies of them all. I wondered how Avery stifled bored yawns. The answer was, of course, she didn't. She yawned in their faces, stepped on their faces, if they were prone, and went her way. What, I wondered, had become of Pritch, in all this time? And what of Tim?

I wondered, that is, until I read the announcement in the *Trib*. Then the *Times*, of course. The *Trib* had Avery's picture. Not a very good one either—no Bachrach. Engaged. They called her a debutante of last season, poor old Avery, who would never be one of any. I wondered if she and Tim would be able to persuade Madre to fill up the snapping-turtle lake again, or had that gone too? How well would *that* nest be feathered? Poor Tim. Poor Avery.

I was very lonely, especially that morning after Mother called up that she was coming home. If Mother was going to die, who would I have left? When my tears had dried, I sat staring forlornly at the phone.

Suddenly I felt like the heroine of that novel—What was it? Some paperback thing—*The Girl with the Glass Heart*. The heroine, a girl named Ellie, was always hoping the phone would ring and someone, a stranger, would say, "Hello. I love you...."

Or had she wanted to pick up the phone and say it herself? I picked up the phone and gave the operator Charles La

Marr's East Hampton number, and when, after centuries, I heard his voice, that's what I said too: "Hello. I love you."

After that it was easy; or now it seems so. Getting my picture in the *Trib* and the *Times* and a word from Nancy Randolph seemed the natural and inevitable culmination to the easiest thing in the world. The "arrangements" went as smoothly as if they had been listed (1) Mother to conquer (three doses of Charles' persuasions); (2) Bart and Joycie to quiet; (3) his friends to meet and gently lower the eyebrows of.

Our "whirlwind engagement" whirled into being in about three weeks. Charles, himself, of course, was the hardest of all. For though he wanted it, he was against it. He acceded, but did not concede. Oddly enough, I think it was Mother who finally got him.

I suppose I will never know what she told him, or what he told her, but it was as if she had willed me to him, and he had no choice. She had always said she believed in early marriages—before Joyce's to Bart had come along—especially for girls. She said it completed the launching that the debut started and the sooner the better. That I was *so* young I think she waived, because she felt I needed Charles, in lieu of her. With her on my side, I was ecstatic, triumphant, and like a tigress in defense of Charles to Bart.

It was a fierce scene. Bart cried like a baby and Joyce literally cursed me for my willful foolishness. "You're going to ruin your damn silly life!" she cried at the top of her lungs.

"He'll be dead before you're really grown up," Bart predicted, suddenly catapulting Charles into the future at a rate of speed exceeding that of light.

"Look at him! Wrinkled and sagging with age," Joyce began on a catalogue of his disqualifications, and I calmly slapped her in the face.

Bart, in turn, slapped me in mine, and not so calmly, and they retired to their torture chambers on the third floor where, I suppose, Bart lulled himself with liquor and Joyce bathed herself in tears of hysteria. Mother, all of this time, was under sedation; a corpse with a flame of life left to feed her heart, sometimes stir her will, and occasionally open the rusty doors of her mind.

The next day I talked to her briefly, though the doctor asked me not to. I had to. I had, once more, to have reassurance. I suppose she only half heard me as I let loose with a flood of emotional and factual reportage, like the town crier wanting to be cued on his performance.

"You think you love him, don't you?" Her voice was as thin as the hand that lay, as unused as a glove, at her side.

"I love him endlessly, and he's right for me, and he's good for me, and we'll go away, just as you told him we ought to, and live in Europe for a while until I really grow up, and he'll teach me to be grown up—"

"Yes, I think he will," she said. "I think he's willing to. Why on earth, I don't know. But I'm glad. I'll tell Bart so again and get him off your neck. And you go on about your business."

"Mother—you really think so?"

She nodded. "It's unreasonable, but if you want it, it's probably right."

That night we thought she was going to die. The doctor said she would, and we sat around and waited. Charles sat with me, in the den, and at last Joyce and Bart stole in and joined us and we sat momentarily united like wild animals on a tree trunk in a roaring flood. We sat all night, and the next morning it cleared again, the sun shone, and Mother awoke wide-eyed, rested, alert.

That was when she told us it should be announced in the paper, so people would know she had given her consent, had wanted it, and that Charles hadn't just taken advantage of my age.

Of course it was awkward. People were embarrassed, as if the Longtrees had made a spectacle of themselves by telescoping the public events of life; according to the rules of decorum, such events should be spread out over a number of quiet, calm years, not crammed into a few months. There was Bart, then Mother's illness and now me—and soon to be the birth of Bart's child. Marriage, death, marriage, birth— and the oddest marriages.

Only they did not seem odd to me. I was completely caught up into Charles' ownership; it could not have been more complete if he had fancied me at the slave mart, bought me, and possessed me. "You don't see him as he is," Joyce's eyes seemed to say each time she saw us together—which was almost constantly. And then I would reappraise him; and find him magnificent, however set apart from the people who formerly had been what I thought of as mine. This also was mine, only a million times more so. If the world wanted to think of him as equivalent to the man from Mars, let them! They didn't have a man from Mars, I did! I knew what it was. I wrote Aunt Maude an incredibly long letter about him, and also wrote Portia.

Of course, it was taken for granted that Charles and I would have no real wedding. We expected nothing from anyone; fanfare of any kind would have been not just horribly wrong, but painful. From here on in, we would move quietly. The date of the wedding was set, for Christmas week, and the wedding itself, it was decided, would be announced afterwards. Charles and I would leave for Europe sometime in January. If Mother…no one finished that sentence.

I spent weekends at East Hampton. Charles' sister, who lived in Oyster Bay, came out with her husband. They were quiet people with thoughtful eyes and we mostly played bridge. Her husband was fond of sailing and when be and Charles talked, it was mostly about that, or about cooking—both of them were marvelous cooks. Gradually, after our engagement was announced, he had his friends in to meet me, one at a time. Of course they wanted a look at me. But they too were quite thoughtful. It seemed all opinions were being reserved. Everything seemed to be held in abeyance; everything was waiting. What for? I asked myself occasionally. But then it was always time for lunch and the excellent omelet Charles had made that I had to inspect first, or time to drive over to so-and-so's for drinks (drinks always meaning two, no more) or time for this, or that.

Everything was noted down and ticked off. It was like

shopping in a sensible, thorough way, and nothing would be judged until later. I knew, or thought, that Charles had all of his people primed, well in hand, firmly controlled. And he controlled me too. He made love to me only twice, in those weeks, and then very discreetly, when no one else could possibly know. Each night he kissed me, and sometimes he held my hand, but mostly he took my hand affectionately, guidingly, when anyone else was around, as if, indeed, he had been told he was to inherit me. I wasn't his yet. Meantime, I was being protected. It was as old-fashioned as the nineteenth century. Unbelievable.

Sometimes, being so close to Southampton, I thought of ringing up Avery. I thought of the mad parties I might ring into, catch her laughing, holding a champagne glass, kissing Tim, as the phone rang, and she would say, "Darling! You crazy mixed-up kid! Ditch him and rush over!" But I didn't want to "ditch him" and "rush over" and watch things "shape up great," as they probably would put it in the mad meadows of Cowledom. I breathed quietly, at his side, waiting. A dog and her master. Then the short list of things done by the hour and on the hour would be over and we would be back in New York, and that was a different matter.

In town, Joyce and I miserably accompanied each other in my search for clothes. This was her mother's idea. Ida Bradford came in town one day and we lunched at the Plaza—her treat—and she advised us, with the utmost tact, to bury our differences. "Chloe will need all sorts of things if she's going to Europe forever," she told us. "Let's all look together now, and then you two can go on from there." That day was a success, but the others weren't. Wanly, we took taxis, because Joyce got too tired to trudge around. And the parcels, even the few I insisted on bringing along, she somehow looked upon as personal afflictions. She lifted hatboxes, against my protests, or little packages from the cab when we reached home as if they were bricks dragged to the site of the pyramids, which she must fit into place. After these sessions, I ran in to look at my mother. Often she was asleep, as they called being in a coma; then, on the verge of tears from aggravation and fright, I would dash back out on the street, hail a cab and drag Charles off to my favorite haunt—a bar around the corner from his office.

Here, we held hands. Or, rather, he held mine, releasing one only to let me lift my drink. He drank too, but seemed sober even when I knew he was dead drunk. He never said anything about what was going on at the moment. All the preliminaries were over, and only time remained. The gap, however badly filled, had to be filled, and he was, as he had been on that first drive into town, wisely wordless. It was Charles who taught me the William Blake poem, *"Never seek to tell thy love, love that never told can be—"* He said the whole of it to me one afternoon, quietly, in answer to the violent protest I made over the madness that had fallen upon us—all of it. I was slightly drunk.

"The world is not 'too much with us, late and soon,'" he said. "It's almost never with us. We won't let it be." Then quickly he began to talk of Europe, as he always did, of all the places we would go, the kind of house we would have, the pair of dogs he planned to buy me. It all seemed peculiar, unreal, but satisfying, as music must be to the terribly wild and disturbed, when it steals over them quietly, without warning.

V

Portia, timorous as an upstairs maid, appeared at the door one morning. For some reason, I was up and let her in myself. "Chloe," she fell on me, her suitcase thudding at her side. "Oh, man!"

I looked at her. She was crying. She took off her glasses and wiped them, still entangled with her pocketbook, her gloves, my outstretched hand. "Can I come in? I mean, may I? Not just for a minute, but maybe—maybe for a week?"

"Of course," I told her. I picked up her fallen suitcase, all covered with school labels and other junk.

We went into the den, and Portia, her hat reinstalled on her head, lifted a hand and pushed it back. Her forehead, this time, was all covered with pimples, red and vicious-looking, but her face was clear. She arranged new-cut bangs over her disfigurement.

"Oh, mother, am I ever glad to be here!" she breathed. "What a life I've led."

Seeing her sitting there, that lousy hat, chosen with her own lousy taste, sitting on her old ugly hair, I could think of

212

nothing but school. I wondered if she could have been expelled.

"You sure it won't be awful, my staying here, with your mother and all—and—well, I mean—"

"Don't," I said.

"Anyway, it won't be for real. I'll just leave things here. To show I'm here. I'm really staying with Petey."

"Petey?"

She nodded. "The most. Chloe, you just don't dig what—" she shook her head. "What I mean is, Petey is the greatest. I'm completely gone. He is. The parents are all drenched with envy and lousy—they just won't—I know it makes no sense."

I told her it didn't, and asked for details. Petey was from her hometown; old, old. He loved her. Ipso facto: she was here. "How old?" I asked.

"Twenty-eight," she said. "Chloe, I couldn't stay at school they'd expel me. You've just got to let me hang on here—hang on until I know what to do."

Twenty-eight! Old! I don't know how long I thought about it, but I thought for a long time, her worried eyes interrupting me whenever they caught me. Little unformed Portia. Smart Portia who didn't know a damned thing. "It's a bad angle," I told her. Then I asked, "Is Petey in town? Staying at the Commodore, or something?"

She nodded. It was all too clear. "And you're going down there and join him?"

She nodded.

I hated her hat. Hated her face. "Joycie will be down

soon. Don't tell her," I said. "Let's just eat breakfast like nature's own."

"I can't!" she gulped, and started crying again.

"Avery's marrying my great gone guy, did you know?" I asked her to stem the tide.

She nodded, but it wasn't stemmed. "And you're marrying an old man to take care of you," she said. "Is that what I'm going to do?"

Kill her? Kill her now, or later? I was plunged to the depths of an unknown sea of horrors, like a lobster scalded to death by the hand of hungry innocence. There I writhed and died, waiting to be devoured by the pure mouth, the young gullet. If I had had a knife I would have plunged it in her stomach. But Bart came in and saved her.

"Joycie's not coming down," he said hurriedly, then, seeing Portia, said, "Why, hello there!" and they made talk while I glared and writhed inside, struggling for the moment of vengeance.

Bart and Portia talked, over breakfast, and she filled her plate again and again, from the things on the sideboard, as if she were in a restaurant. I loathed her, couldn't wait for Bart to leave. But he stayed, enjoying her young company. At last he left.

"You hate me," she said, while we were still in the dining room and Tennie, cautiously eavesdropping, was removing the dishes from the table.

I bowed my head. "You're detestable," I said.

"I don't mean to be."

"That's too bad."

"I can't go back to Chalmers. I'm too wild about Petey."

"That's your mess," I said. "Leave me to mine."

"Is it a mess?"

"Of course not."

"How's your mother?"

"Oh, you idiot!" I shrieked at her. "You perfect idiot!"

"You want me to go?" she asked, her voice as small as her smallest skin blemish.

"I never wanted you to come!" I cried in rage. "Go back to Chalmers and be expelled! It's better, believe me, it's better!"

"Done," she said. She got up from the table, and I watched her. My eyes followed her. I knew she was perfectly prepared to leave because I had told her to.

"Stay," I said. "Stay and tell me the whole thing."

We went upstairs to my room and she laid out her pathetic wardrobe—her idea of things for a clandestine love affair, a possible honeymoon. I was so upset I offered her things of mine—we were relatively the same size. She cooed over them. She reminded me of Joyce, as she had been when she and Bart were first engaged.

"Do you think he really loves me?" she asked, after she had told me the whole tale—it ran from Seattle to Deauville.

"Yes," I said with no opinion at all. It didn't seem to matter. Life, love—it all seemed so common then. Avery. Portia. Joyce. How different they all were. And Charles, my Charles. But I could not think of him. He was set apart from the others.

"I want you to meet Petey—urgently," she said. "I've arranged it."

It struck me then, as never before, how selfish people were: what made her think I could leave my mother, or leave my Charles, having left my mother, for her Petey—and her? I wanted to choke her for her beastliness. What made her think I was interested, could be?

My impassioned recital stilled her: I told her about what was happening, here in this house, to my mother, how she was dying—I spared no details. I made her see how inconvenient her visit was. I told her about my quiet life with Charles, his acceptance, the waiting. In short, I exposed her selfishness for her. "You think," I finished off, "that because *you* have found love, at the age of fifteen—or whatever you are—"

"Sixteen," I was corrected.

"—that you must have it all. Have it, but have it somewhere else."

"I offered to go." she said.

Then I was sorry. I said so. "I'm the same," I told her.

"We're all the same," she told me.

That night, I suppose, Portia went off and slept with her Petey. Anyway, it was not until two nights later that "the meeting" took place. Petey, she said, wanted to meet "us." Charles was reluctant, having met Portia herself by then. I don't know why I insisted, but I did.

That night, for some reason, before we went out, I went in to Mother. It was before Charles arrived, and Portia had fled out to meet her beloved. I think I wanted to talk to

Mother, but, as usual now, she lay there like Snow White under glass, dead. Awful as it may seem, we had gotten used to her that way: only an occasional quiver, a rare conscious hour, proved she was still alive. But I watched her; I didn't want her to die. I don't think I believed she ever would.

I stood there at the foot of the hospital bed installed in place of her own, since it was easier for the nurse, and looked down at that being who had been my mother, and was all I had left for one. It came to me then that it really was over: no more flash messages from the flesh that was past—now I was on my own.

Charles came while I was still in there. Tennie was with him when I came out. "Mr. Charles says it's cold out, Miss Chloe," she said, and draped an unattractive coat over my shoulders. I was furious.

"Must you be so impatient with her?" he asked me.

I felt the question needed no answer, but by way of one I threw the coat from the cab. I knew it shocked him. "You hate me like this, don't you?" I asked him.

He was silent, as silent as always when a question needs no answer.

"I need a drink," I said, and imperiously leaned forward and told the driver to stop at the next bar.

We dismissed the cab and went in. It was a dirty bar. "I must excuse myself," Charles told me, presently. "But I can't take you with me and I can't leave you alone."

"Leave me alone," I said.

I was wandering around outside when he found me. I looked at him, but I couldn't tell what he thought: I'd had three stingers in there.

Then we went to meet Petey and Portia at the Stork Club—Petey's choice. "I hate this place," I said over and over in the cab, and was still saying it as we walked in the door. "Is he trying to make television, do you think?"

We found them without trouble. Portia was conspicuous, as usual, just for herself, and Petey was something else. He was immaculate and emasculated; he wore dinner clothes and an imperious frown above his cool smile. We were presented, and I sank, rather than sat down, and out of one eye, studied Petey. What was he doing with Portia anyway?

But again, I was in love with Charles. I groped for his hand, found it; cool, there. That was all.

They talked; we didn't. I looked at Petey.

"I think you should go home," Charles told me.

"I think I shouldn't," I said, finishing my drink at a gulp.

If I say that from here in, it all fell into place, I suppose I'd be oversimplifying. But there was Petey. There was Portia. And Charles. Can I say his golden wings molted? No. They turned to gilt. And this happened long before Avery and Tim came in; long before Pritch and Mary Barkley got up to dance and saw us. Petey, Portia had said, was old; but Charles— how can I describe how I came back to my youth? It hadn't been Shangri-la—he didn't crumble into a powder as he came down off the mountain. He sat there, sedate, endearing, but full of hatred, disapproval: I knew with a terrible knowledge that I would be changed, if I were ever truly to become his. We would descend to the bowels of the earth, an unknown cellar, and I would be strapped upon a table to be transformed: I would be remade, by Charles, into his Patsy. I was horribly frightened, he looked at me with such inexorably possessive eyes, eyes that said, "You're mine, you know."

Tim. Avery. His eyes, her eyes, were full of sadness. They brimmed over our table. "We love you," they told me—their eyes—separately, and together. Then there was Pritch. He stumbled with what he felt. He asked me my phone number again, as if he had lost it, or as if he had never had it. And no one looked at Charles. He sat among us like a handsome unnoticed doll in a nursery of screaming children. I should have looked at him even if the others didn't—that much, at least, I could have done, but my sense of loyalty and fairness were outweighed by cowardice and premature guilt over what I knew was coming. It was as if he were an old beloved pet dog, soon to be shot, to whom I could not offer even the comfort of a good-by.

Pritch yanked me up to dance to "When the Saints Go Marching In"—always one of his favorites, one of his irresistibles. I'd danced a lot to that with him. It was really like being home. We rubbed noses and giggled, and Avery yanked the ribbon off my pony-tail as we bumped into them. Timmy took it away from her and held it under his nose for a mustache.

As I was laughing I realized my lungs felt as if they had opened up for the first time in weeks. I felt wild with exhilaration, as if I had been let out of a vast stuffy room. Eagerly, I turned to Pritch, pulled him down into the empty chair beside mine. We talked. We talked and talked and talked, and then they came around to us to say they were closing. "Come back home with me," I whispered.

"I will," he said.

And only then do I think I realized that Charles had gone.

That was a long time ago—two weeks. And Pritch is away, and I will soon be away too. But it was all right. Charles has gone. He sent a telegram. Unnecessary. And Mother just hangs on, but by bits and pieces, not fits and starts—it can't last. And I know it. I know it. And here I am. No Charles. No Bart—he thinks it's awful—not even Pritch. Nothing but the wide, wide future—wide as the sky, Charles would say—wide as God, Pritch would say—wide as the grave, Mother would say—but wide; everyone agrees it is wide. And here I am. I think I know how it will narrow down. I've written Charles an "I'm sorry" letter. And, most of all, I've written me a "Dear Seventeen" letter—

...Next year, thank God, I'll be older....